J. T. EDSON'S
FLOATING OUTFIT

The toughest bunch of Rebels that ever lost a war, they fought for the South, and then for Texas, as the legendary Floating Outfit of "Ole Devil" Hardin's O.D. Connected ranch.

MARC COUNTER was the best-dressed man in the West: always dressed fit-to-kill. BELLE BOYD was as deadly as she was beautiful, with a "Manhattan" model Colt tucked under her long skirts. THE YSABEL KID was Comanche fast and Texas tough. And the most famous of them all was DUSTY FOG, the ex-cavalryman known as the Rio Hondo Gun Wizard.

J. T. Edson has captured all the excitement and adventure of the raw frontier in this magnificent Western series. Turn the page for a complete list of Berkley Floating Outfit titles.

GOODNIGHT'S DREAM

BERKLEY BOOKS, NEW YORK

GOODNIGHT'S DREAM

A Berkley Book / published by arrangement with
the author

PRINTING HISTORY
First published in Great Britain in 1969
Robert Hale edition / October 1978
Berkley edition / June 1980

ISBN: 0-425-04633-8

A BERKLEY BOOK® TM 757,375

PRINTED IN THE UNITED STATES OF AMERICA

For "Boot-Neck"
George Meadows

ONE

Give 'em a Texas-sized Gutful

Toward noon the three riders passed down the eastern rim, waded their horses across the Pecos River and turned downstream, heading southward. They were tall men dressed in travel-stained range clothing, with Army Colts holstered on their belts and rifles in their saddle boots. Despite their apparently relaxed air, they were alertly cautious as became travelers in a potentially hostile land. The man closest to the river led a pack mule which carried their bed rolls and supplies. Of the three, he showed the greatest signs of watchfulness. Eyes constantly scanning the sloping, bush-dotted, rock-speckled land to the west, he broke the trio's silence with a comment.

"Colonel Charlie allowed we should only ride at night, boss."

"That was only if there's Indians about," answered the man in the center of the group. Tanned like his companions and no better dressed, he bore himself with an air of one used to leadership. He was Oliver Loving, pioneer cattleman from Texas and part-owner of a trail herd some thirty miles behind him. "We haven't seen a sign of them and time's running short. The Army're letting out their beef contracts at Fort Sumner and I want to be on hand when they start."

"Figure it'll be worth us getting it, boss?" inquired the second cowhand. "The beef contract from the Yankees, I mean."

"It'll be worth getting," Loving confirmed. "Like Charl—"

"Boss!" interrupted the first speaker, reining in his horse and pointing.

Some thirty or more figures appeared on the skyline about two hundred yards ahead of the Texans. Stocky, thickset men wearing clothing made mainly from the hides of pronghorn antelope and sitting their horses with an almost effortless casual grace. Swiftly Loving studied the newcomers, noting the lack of eagle feather headdresses, that all of them had the appearance of youth and only six at most carried firearms.

Young or not, one of the six acted with speed and decision. Dropping from his wiry horse, he lit down kneeling and cradled the butt of a tack-decorated Sharps rifle against his right shoulder. He landed on the ground, took aim and fired all in a single flowing movement to make a mighty unlucky hit from Loving's point of view: lead ploughed into the rancher's horse. Feeling the impact and his mount beginning to go down, Loving thrust himself clear of the collapsing animal. On landing, he slid the Henry rifle from its saddleboot and barked out his orders.

A skilled fighting man and well versed in Indian warfare, the rancher knew what must be done. There was no hope of escaping the fleet-footed Indian horses riding double or leading the pack-mule, but across the river a short way from where he stood, he saw the mouth of a cave in the wall of the rim. From it he could make a stand and hope to hold off the Indians until help arrived.

"Leave the mule and go get Colonel Charlie!" Loving ordered.

"Like hell!" replied the man with the mule, guessing what his boss had in mind. "I'm sticking with you. Take off, Spat. We'll try to hold 'em off you."

Much as he hated the thought of leaving the other two, the man called Spat knew it to be their only hope of salvation. A lone, well-mounted man might outride the Indians and fetch help. So he whirled his horse around and started it running.

On the heels of the first shot, the Indians sent their horses leaping forward. Six of them cut away at an angle in pursuit of the fleeting Spat, but the rest made for the dismounted Loving. He fired, flicked down the loading lever and touched off another shot. The leading brave slid from his horse's back and a second warrior veered his mount around violently as a bullet sliced into his shoulder.

"Head for the cave, Sid!" Loving snapped, altering his aim and firing again. "I'll be right after you."

"Yo!" the cowhand answered, turning his horse in the required direction and throwing a malevolent scowl at the mule. "Don't fuss me, you blasted knob-head, or I'll gut you and leave you for the buzzards."

Riding through the water, Sid heard the continuing crackle of the Henry's fire and wondered what the attackers made of it. With Texas left impoverished by the end of the War between the States, few Henry or Spencer rifles had so far made their appearance. So the Indians would not be accustomed to a rifle capable of sustained fire without reloading. Maybe the effect would be sufficient to make them believe their war-medicine had gone sour and they would call off the attack. Knowing the band and nation to which they belonged, Sid doubted if his "maybe" would bear fruit. Certainly he could hear no abating of the attack as the horse and mule splashed through the water. Riding on, he urged the animals into the mouth of the cave, dropped the horse's reins as a means of preventing it from straying and leapt from the saddle. Jerking his Sharps carbine from its saddleboot, he darted to the cave's entrance to support his boss.

Maybe the Indians had never seen a repeating rifle, but they knew about double-barreled weapons and six-shooting revolvers. So at first they showed no great concern when Loving continued to shoot. Not until a fourth buck was knocked from his horse and eight shots had been fired without the ride-plenty* showing signs of having to reload did the implications begin to strike them.

With a couple of bullets hissing by his head, Loving backed toward the river. None of the other firearm toting bucks showed the first's skill and he was still on the rim reloading his weapon. Nor, with over a hundred yards between them, did the remainder of the Indians try to use their bows. Up closer the short, powerful weapons would be more deadly than the

---

*Ride-plenty: Indians' name for Texas cowboys.

rifles, in hands trained from early childhood in their use.

Three more times, as fast as he could work the lever, Loving fired. Then he saw the braves whirling their horses around with superb riding skill, to dash back the way they had come. Wasting no time in self-congratulation, the rancher turned and waded at all speed across the Pecos. A bullet ripped the Stetson from his head as he sprinted over the sand. From the mouth of the cave, Sid's carbine spat in reply. As Loving entered, the cowhand gave him a grin and nodded toward the other side of the river.

"That's give 'em a Texas-sized gutful, boss," he commented with satisfaction. "I wish I'd got that jasper with the rifle. He shoots real good for an Injun."

"Sure," Loving agreed. "If they was anything but *Kweharehnuh* I'd say we'd done enough to scare 'em off. Not Antelope-band Comanches, though. Losing them four'll just make the others more eager to get us."

"Ain't so many of 'em left," Sid remarked.

"They'll soon enough call up help and be back," the rancher replied.

Even as Loving spoke, he saw two of the braves disappear beyond the rim. The rest of the party gathered around the man with the Sharps and began to talk. They would be planning their next move, which meant the defense must be organized and fast.

While larger than the entrance suggested, the cave offered only one way out. Not a serious consideration under the circumstances, as they could only leave after the Comanches departed. In addition to food and ammunition on the pack-mule, they had two large canteens filled with water. So they had the means to hold out until help arrived—assuming that Spat evaded his pursuers and reached the trail herd.

"What're they doing, Sid?" Loving inquired as he went to the waiting animals.

"Still sat talking. Must be more of 'em around, there's smoke coming up back of the rim."

Swinging around, Loving saw the smoke rising. It went up in regulated puffs, not as a single, natural column. If the braves expected reinforcements, they would be unlikely to attack before the others came.

"Watch 'em while I tend to the packs, Sid," Loving said. "Especially that bastard who shot my horse. He can handle a rifle real good."

"That's for—" Sid began, giving his attention to the Indians. "Damn it! He's not among the rest of 'em—"

At which point the brave with the Sharps once more made his presence felt. From behind a clump of black chaparral which looked hardly large enough to hide a jack-rabbit, the rifle banged. Screaming in pain, Sid's horse went down kicking and the mule reared on its hind legs in an attempt to tear free from the stricken animal.

Grabbing the mule's lead rope with his left hand, Loving tried to restrain it. Knowing the consequences should the animal escape, Sid prepared to assist his boss. Before he could do so, he found other matters to hold his attention.

"They're coming again!" the cowhand yelled, exchanging his Sharps in favor of the 1860 Army Colt's six-shot capacity.

Discarding the mule, Loving bounded to the entrance. Once again the Henry started to crack, although its user was painfully aware of its rapidly emptying magazine. However, the Comanche had already been given a taste of repeating fire and learned their lesson. They spun their horses in rump-scraping circles and galloped back up the rim.

Still terrified, the mule fought against its lead rope

and was almost free when a cursing Sid left his post to run toward it, and Loving joined him. Between them, they managed to free the pack-saddle and let it fall to the ground. Then they released the mule, watching it stampede from the cave and go crow-hopping off along the edge of the river.

"Damned good riddance! I hope the Comanches get you and eat you. It'd serve you and them right!" Sid yelled after the departing beast. "Where in hell did Colonel Charlie get that fool knob-head from, boss?"

"John Chisum gave it to him as boot for the cattle deal they made."

"Figures," Sid sniffed. "Chisum'd never've parted with it was it any danged use at all."

"That's for sure," Loving admitted. "But he can supply us with the cattle we need to fill an Army contract should we get one."

Side refrained from expressing further thoughts on Chisum. While the man in question had not yet gained his title of "The Cattle King," he already showed the manner in which he would rise to fame. Sid felt he personally would rather not depend on the shifty-eyed, if jovial-seeming Chisum to supply the stock. However, it was the bosses' affair. One of the blessings remaining to an ordinary cowhand was that Sid did not need to worry about such things.

Even if Loving had felt inclined to discuss Chisum's shortcomings, it was neither the time nor place to do so. Instead there were preparations to be made against a resumption of hostilities.

Crossing to the pack-saddle, Loving removed and opened his bed roll. From the war bag he extracted a box of cartridges for the rifle. The crack of a shot, mingling with the vicious "spang" as a bullet ricocheted from the walls, drew his attention to the door.

"I knowed that young cuss with the rifle'd get hurt if

he went on the way he was going," Sid remarked, lowering his smoking carbine. "He won't be worrying us no more."

"Good," Loving answered, for none of the other braves showed an equal skill with his firearm.

Sitting with his back against the wall, Loving rested the Henry's butt on the ground. Drawing the catch under the magazine toward the muzzle, he compressed the loading spring and opened the tube. With the spring's catch held in its slot, he dropped sufficient flat-nosed B. Tyler Henry .44 rimfire bullets down the tube to replace those already expended. With the magazine full, he turned the tube back into place under the barrel and lowered the head of the spring on to the uppermost round. With his rifle once more holding sixteen bullets, he changed places and allowed Sid to gather ammunition.

While watching the other slope, Loving silently cursed his luck. So far all the attackers appeared to be *tuivitsi*, young and inexperienced warriors. However, if he knew the *Kweharehnuh*, the smoke-signals ought to bring *tehnap* on the run; seasoned braves with battle savvy and capable of planning future attacks with more skill than had so far been shown. So the defenders faced a long, hard struggle and, despite its advantages, the cave was far from impregnable. Even if Spat had made good his escape and reached the herd, help might not arrive in time. In fact, Goodnight could muster at most twenty men. A small enough force to take on a band of Antelope Comanches.

There was another aspect to disturb Loving. Against his partner's advice, he had insisted on pushing ahead of the herd so as to reach Fort Sumner more quickly than would be possible accompanying the cattle. The earlier he arrived, Loving had figured, the greater his chance of picking up a lucrative contract to supply the Army with beef needed to feed and hold the Apache Indians peacably on the reservations.

While Goodnight agreed with the possibility, he also saw the dangers of a small party making the journey. Before finally agreeing, he had asked Loving to travel only by night. Although Loving began by intending to follow the advice, seeing no sign of Indians led him to indiscretion. Jumped by the *Kweharehnuh*, his arrival at Fort Sumner would be at least delayed if not canceled entirely under the Pecos rim. In the latter case, Loving hoped that Spat would reach Goodnight. Even if Charlie failed to save his partner, he would know of Loving's fate and not continue the drive.

"Some more of 'em come up, boss," Sid remarked, joining his employer. "They're sure talking up a storm there."

"Likely the *tuivitsi* 're telling the others about my Henry," Loving guessed. "I'd say them fellers who've just come'll have to see if it's true."

Verification of the rancher's assumption came swiftly. Most of the newcomers let out challenging war whoops and charged down the slope. Wanting to impress them with his rifle's firepower, Loving started shooting fast. Some bullets flew in reply, striking the wall around the entrance or whining into the cave. At a hundred yards from the river, with two braves down and a couple more wounded, the attackers turned aside. Scooping up their fallen companions, they returned to the rim amid jeers and comments from the first party.

If Loving hoped that a further reverse would send the *Kweharehnuh* on their way, he was disappointed. Although they withdrew, the braves went no farther than the top of the rim. Dismounting, they gathered about the senior warrior present and listened to his advice. Then men armed with rifles found positions from which they could cover the cave's mouth. The rest took the horses out of sight. Clearly they were prepared for a long siege.

There were no further attacks made that day. Nor did the watchers waste lead and powder by shooting at the cave. More braves came at intervals, including a warbonnet chief and many *tehnap*. Loving and Sid knew the Comanches would not give up without further attempts to dislodge them.

"What do you reckon, boss?" Sid inquired as the sun sank toward the western rim.

"Likely they'll try to jump us at dawn," the rancher replied. "It's a full moon tonight, so we'll be able to see if they try sneaking up too close."

"With the moon we can't chance slipping out," Sid remarked. "Might've tried to get by 'em and to their horses but for that."

"Not a hope of it," Loving grunted. "They're *Kweharehnuh*, not a bunch of Mission Tejases. We *could* take a whirl at going up the rim on this side but we'd be a-foot come morning and they'd have found out we'd gone."

"I surely hates walking," Sid declared. "'Specially when the fellers after me's got hosses. Looks like it's root, hog or die right here until Colonel Charlie comes to fetch us out."

"That's what we'll do," Loving agreed.

Although aware that the Comanche did not normally attack at night—figuring that *Ka-Dih,* the Great Spirit, might not find the soul of a warrior killed in the darkness—the Texans took no chances. While Sid made up a meal of biscuits, pemmican and water,

Loving watched the slope. Then they alternated a constant guard as the night went by. With the land before them illuminated by a bright full moon, they could see the Pecos well enough to detect any attempt to sneak up on them.

Apart from the glow of fires beyond the rim and the occasional coming and going of braves watching the cave's entrance, there was no sign of activity from the Comanches.

Sitting with his back against the wall and his Sharps carbine resting on his knees, Sid was waiting out the last hour or so before sun-up. Soon he would wake up his boss so that Loving could make preparations to meet the attack when it came.

A faint scuffling clicking noise from above drew Sid's attention from the slope. Something fell, clattering lightly to the ground before the entrance. Sid tensed slightly as he saw the thing which disturbed him. A few small rocks had fallen from the rim over the cave. Which meant somebody was up there—and that somebody must be the Comanches. Sid wondered what the Indians hoped to achieve from their new position. Rising sheer for a good forty feet, the wall could not be climbed. So the braves on top posed little threat to the defenders. Most likely they were a newly arrived group who were surveying the situation before joining the main body.

"Boss!" Sid hissed, figuring that Loving would want to know about the arrivals.

Stirring in his blankets, Loving sat up and looked around. Then he rose with the Henry in his hand and joined the other man at the entrance.

"Anything doing?"

"Not across the river, but I thought I heard something on the rim."

"Cover me!" Loving ordered, then moved cautiously out of the cave.

Looking up, the rancher could see no sign of life on the rim. His thoughts ran parallel to Sid's on the matter and he withdrew to shelter as a rifle cracked on the opposite slope, its bullet whining off the wall above his head.

"Couldn't see anything up there," the rancher stated on his return. "And there's no way they could climb down near enough to do them any good."

"The chief's on the other side," Sid answered. "Maybe come to see what the shooting's about. It won't be long now."

"That's for sure," admitted Loving. "Unless they call it off now they know they can't take us by surprise with a dawn rush."

"If they do hold off, Colonel Charlie ought to be getting here afore long."

"And running into odds of maybe ten to one. You can't stack up against that many *Kweharehnuh* and hope to come out of it winning."

"Which won't stop Colonel Charlie trying," Sid said. "We'd best hope that we can down enough of 'em so they'll reckon their medicine's all ways bad when our boys get here."

Nodding grimly, Loving inched himself forward until he could look along the wall of the rim in each direction. Despite the area being in shadow, he found no signs of the Comanche having sent braves across the river to stalk the cave entrance on foot ready to attack when the main body made their assault.

Slowly the sun crept up and the dawn's greyness lessened by the second. On the rim, the chief and many braves sat their horses. At an order from their leader, the warriors armed with rifles opened fire on the cave.

Then the mounted men swept forward in a fast-moving line. Leaving their places of concealment, the men with the rifles bounded on to the mounts led to them by companions. Down the slope thundered the savage warriors, yelling their war-whoops and exhibiting no caution or concern at the idea of facing the repeating rifle.

"Give 'em hell, Sid!" Loving ordered, lining his Henry.

Whipping the carbine to his shoulder, Sid extended the barrel of the Sharps beyond the mouth of the cave. Two brown hands flashed into view from the wall at the entrance, grasping the barrel and giving a savage heave at it. Taken by surprise, Sid was jerked forward and fired the Sharps only to see its bullet throw up sand on the nearer bank of the stream. Unable to stop himself, the cowhand stumbled into the open and fell to his knees. Releasing the carbine after dragging its owner into sight, a Comanche brave snatched the tomahawk from his belt. Around whistled the sharp blade, biting into Sid's skull and tumbling him to the ground.

An instant later the brave also died. Swiveling around Loving drove a bullet into the center of the savage, paint-decorated face. Even as the Comanche went over backward, another brave came into sight but from Loving's side of the entrance. Swiftly the rancher swung his rifle, working the lever as fast as he could, and fired with the muzzle almost touching the buck's chest. Thrown backward by the impact, the Indian fell under the feet of two more braves as they leapt from the way he had come.

Loving's thoughts on how so many *Kweharehnuh* had managed to cross the river and reach the wall flanking the entrance undetected received a rapid answer. Coiling down from above, a rope's end descended before the mouth of the cave and agitated violently. Following the rope, a pair of legs slid into view, followed by the all but naked body of a *tuivitsi*. At the crack of the Henry, the young buck released the rope and crashed down.

Everything was clear to the rancher. During the night, the chief had sent men across the Pecos out of the defender's range of vision to climb the rim. When ready for the attack to begin, the men made their descent on ropes taken for that purpose. It was a smart notion, worthy of a war chief of the Antelope Comanche. Not even the rapid-fire qualities of the Henry could save Loving, for more warriors appeared and the rope before him seemed to be alive as other braves started to climb down.

Retreating, Loving prepared to sell his life dearly. Flame lashed from the Navy Colt held by one of the Comanches and the rancher felt lead burn into him. He reeled back a pace, the left hand dropping numb and limp to his side. Even as he let the rifle fall and grabbed at his holstered Colt, a second brave sent an arrow flashing into the cave. Pain ripped into Loving as the arrow sliced between his ribs. Staggering, he felt his legs buckle and he went down.

TWO

I've Lost a Real Good Friend

Despite the importance of the herd of cattle to the fulfillment of his plans, Charles Goodnight did not hesitate when Spat rode up with news of Loving's predicament. Nor did the fact that he might have excellent means of effecting a rescue in any way influence his decision, although having half a troop of Cavalry and a battery of Mountain Artillery along— they had arrived an hour after Loving's departure— gave Goodnight a greater chance of saving his partner and friend.

In some ways Goodnight resembled a Comanche, being thickset for his five-foot nine inches of height and exhibiting a similar effortless grace when on the back of a horse. However, from his low-crowned, wide-brimmed white Stetson to his spur-heeled, star-decorated boots, his appearance said Texas cattleman. Instead of the usual calf-skin vest, he wore one made from the rosette-dotted hide of a jaguar which, having strayed north from Mexico, made the mistake of killing some of his cattle. Around his waist hung a gunbelt supporting matched rosewood-handled 1860 Army Colts in contoured holsters. From under his left leg showed the butt of a Henry rifle. His tanned face, with its grizzled brown beard, was set in grim lines as he rode his *bayo-cebrunos** gelding toward the two Army officers.

When they heard Goodnight's news and intentions, the officers showed their willingness to help with the rescue. Like many of their kind, they had small love for Texans but Major Lane of the Artillery and 1st Lieutenant Leonard in charge of the Cavalry escort saw the possibilities of being involved. With promotion all but stagnant since the end of the War, even a moderately successful operation against a band of hostile Indians would bring them to the all-important notice of their superiors.

That especially applied to Lane. A career Artillery officer, he had been sent west with his battery to help fight the Apaches in New Mexico. Texas had Indian problems too, but the Territory of New Mexico supported the Union during the War between the States and so received priority over the rebel Lone Star State. While the appointment had advantages, it also carried problems. Command in New Mexico rested in the hands of Cavalry officers, who naturally meant to see that their arm of the service received every benefit. Mountain artillery had been used during the War, but

---

* *Bayo-cebrunos:* a dun color shading into smoky grey.

not in a major action or decisively enough for its capabilities to become generally known. Lane saw the advantages of reaching Fort Sumner with a victory to his credit. He would find the commanding officer at the Fort more amenable if he brought news that his guns had already routed a band of marauding Indians.

"I'll have my men ready to march—" Lane began.

"We're going to have to travel real fast, Major," Goodnight interrupted. "Was I you, I'd just take your three best gun-crews and fastest mules. John!"

"Yo!" replied the rancher's tall, lean and leathery-tough segundo.

"Send all but—eight with me," Goodnight ordered, pausing to decide how small a group he might safely leave to handle the cattle. "Reckon you can keep the herd moving with just eight?"

"I'll sure as hell try," John Poe answered. "Spat's just told me about Oliver and Sid. He allows to ride back with you. I've got the wrangler fetching up a fresh horse for him."

No less aware than Lane of the opportunities, Leonard put in, "My men'll be ready to ride in fifteen minutes, Mr. Goodnight."

"*I'll* take half of them while you command the rest here and escort the remainder of my battery," Lane corrected, not meaning to share any glory with a Cavalryman if he could help it. "Sergeant Major! One, Three and Five guns, four ammunition mules. I want two carrying solid shot, two with a spherical case. Move it."

"Yo!" answered the sergeant major and galloped off to obey.

"Keep with the cattle until we rejoin you, Mr. Leonard," Lane commanded. "In fifteen minutes, Mr. Goodnight."

"We'll be ready," the rancher promised.

Knowing the serious nature of the situation, everybody concerned with the rescue attempt worked fast. Goodnight selected a powerful roan stallion, fast, with endurance to spare and steady in any kind of emergency. All the cowhands also picked from their mount—no Texan said "string" for his team of work horses—animals suited to long, hard riding.

Within fifteen minutes all was ready. Having learned the need for mobility by fighting against the superb Confederate States cavalry, Lane's men were all mounted, instead of working on foot as was usual among Mountain Artillery batteries. From the way they handled their horses, Goodnight concluded Lane's men had been well trained.

Fifteen Texans, twenty-five cavalrymen and the crews for the three howitzers carried on six mules followed Goodnight and Lane away from the herd. The cavalrymen were armed with Army Colts and Springfield carbines, while the gunners wore revolvers only. Every Texan carried at least one revolver and a rifle or carbine of some description, although very few owned repeaters.

After watching Goodnight depart, John Poe swung to the waiting cowhands. He saw that the herd had been deserted, which was not what his boss wanted to happen.

"Get them cattle moving!" Poe bawled.

"Just us?" yelped a cowhand, for only eight of the actual trail crew remained. The cook and his louse were needed to drive the chuck and bedwagons, while the two wranglers left by Goodnight would be fully occupied with handling the remuda of reserve horses.

"Naw!" Poe spat back. "There's half of the blasted Texas Light Cavalry coming up to lend a hand. Move it. Head 'em up and keep 'em going!"

Whirling their horses, the cowhands dashed to the herd. Watching them, Poe wondered if such a small body of men could deal with the fifteen hundred head of longhorn steers.

Much the same thoughts ran through Goodnight's head and he wondered if he had done the right thing by telling his segundo to keep the herd moving. If anything happened to the cattle, he and Loving would be in bad shape financially. That did not worry Goodnight for himself, but Loving had a wife and children dependent on the success of the trail drive. Of course, the loss of the herd would mean that Goodnight would have to try some other method to make his dream come true.

Riding through potentially hostile country to a friend's rescue was neither the time nor place to think of schemes for the future, important as they might be. So Goodnight put them from his mind and concentrated on the work in hand. At his suggestion, a pair of men skilled in such matters rode ahead as scouts.

All too well Goodnight knew the Comanche Nation. While a loyal Texan, he had declined to fight for the South during the War. Instead he had given his services for the benefit of the State by being a member of Captain Jack Cureton's company of Texas Rangers. Acting as Cureton's chief scout—the title 'Colonel' being honorary, granted in respect for his fighting ability and integrity—Goodnight had learned much about the *Nemenuh*.* So he realized the danger and knew that, unless Loving and Sid had been killed before reaching the shelter of the cave, other

---

*Nemenuh: "The People," the Comanches' name for their nation.

Kweharehnuh warriors would gather fast to share in sport and spoils. By the time the rescue party arrived, there might be a large number of the hard-fighting Comanche braves present. If so, Goodnight did not want them to be warned of his coming.

To give them their due, the soldiers could handle their horses and mules real well. Veterans of the War, they knew how to travel fast for long periods and did not delay the Texans as the latter feared they might with the howitzers along. Ordinary horse artillery, drawing their guns and limbers along on wheels, could not have kept pace with the mounted men across the range country. The mules, specially selected for their work, carried their disassembled lightweight howitzers at a speed equal to that of the horses.

On they rode, not even night's arrival causing them to slow their pace. The scouts saw no sign of the braves who had pursued Spat, so Goodnight concluded they *had* returned to the main attack force. Nor did the *Kweharehnuh* appear to have taken the trouble to send out scouts. Probably they had assumed that the three white men did not belong to a larger body and that Spat had fled to save his life at the expense of his companions.

Reaching the rim above the Pecos, Spat announced that they were within two miles of where he had left Loving and Sid.

"I can't hear any shooting," Lane said as the cowhand finished speaking. "Surely we should by now."

"It's not likely," Goodnight replied. "Unless there's no way of avoiding it, Comanches don't fight at night."

"Maybe they're not around any more," Lane suggested, just a hint of disappointment in his voice.

"If they're not, Major," Goodnight answered coldly,

"I've lost a real good friend. This's *Kweharehnuh* country and they're like bulldogs in a fight. Once they take hold, they stick until they're killed or it's over."

"What do you suggest?" Lane asked in a low tone. While willing to accept advice from an authority on Indian fighting, he did not want his men to know that he requested it.

"Was it me, I'd have the trail hands and at least half the horse-soldiers down there on the other side of the river and you up here with your guns where you can see what you're shooting at. Soon's we see the Comanches, we'll let you toss a couple of cannon balls at 'em, then go in like the devil-after-a-yearling."

"We'll toss more than just a couple, and there'll be case shot among them, seventy-eight musket balls apiece."

"That's your side of it, Major," Goodnight said. "Let's get moving and find a place for my bunch to go down."

Nodding agreement, Lane hid his surprise at discovering the rancher's appreciation of how to handle the affair. Of course, many Texans had served in the Confederate Army and he recalled having heard the cowhands address Goodnight as "Colonel."

After riding on a short way, they found a place down which Goodnight's part of the force could reach the river. Many anxious glances were directed by the Texans toward the eastern horizon, for they knew what dawn would mean if Loving and Sid should still be alive. Descending, they crossed the river and followed Goodnight along the west bank of the Pecos.

It was Lane's party who saw the Comanche first. They were approaching a point where the valley made a bend that hid the Indians from the men at the lower level. Bringing his horse to a halt, Lane stared to where the braves had gathered at the head of the opposite slope. Trained eyes studied the scene and made various rapid calculations.

"Action front!" Lane barked to his waiting men. "Eight hundred and eighty yards. Load and commence firing."

Even while the words were being spoken, the trained crews started to move. Leaping from their horses and tossing the reins to the waiting cavalrymen, they ran to the mules. Swiftly the wheels and carriages were unshipped from the mules which carried them and assembled. Even as nuts were being tightened to secure the pieces, the tube was brought from its carrier and fitted into position. Other men unloaded and opened the ammunition panniers, two from each mule, lifting the lids to expose the eight rounds each held.

"Three-and-three-quarter-second fuse!" ordered the sergeant in charge of the ammunition supply, estimating the time it would take for a spherical case shell to reach its destination half a mile away.

Obediently the men from One and Three guns cut into the circular pewter disc of a case shell's Borman fuse at the appropriate place. Then they carried their charges to the guns. Having no need for such refinements as fuses, the Five gun was first into action. Taking the fixed round from the man who brought it, the loader tore the paper covering from the serge powder bag and slid the charge down the 32.9-inch-long tube. Another man used the vent-pick to pierce the powder bag, leaving a clear way for the flame from the friction primer* to reach the waiting explosive charge. Pushing the primer into place, he connected it

---

*A description of how a friction primer works is given in *The Hooded Riders*.

to the lanyard and backed clear of the howitzer.

"Trail left!" ordered the gunner, having set the tube for the desired angle to hurl the solid shot among the Indians. "Right a shade! A touch more! Steady! Fire!"

Within one minute of Lane's command, the Number Five howitzer boomed out its first shot. Five seconds later, the One and Three guns spoke and their loads rose skyward following the solid shot's curving arc toward where the Indians had already begun their attack down the slope.

Plunging out of the heavens, the solid shot hurled up a cloud of sand from the west bank of the river. Ignited by the detonating main powder charge, a spurt of flame crept along the Borman fuse of each spherical case shell. At best using case shell, even with the well-designed Borman fuses, was a chancy business, with premature bursts, or no detonation at all occurring regularly. The case from the One howitzer exploded some thirty feet in the air over the Comanches, raining .69 caliber musket balls down on them. While set for the same time, the other case landed ahead of the attacking braves before the flame crawling along the fuse reached and ignited the 4.5-ounce burster charge. However, the crew of the Three gun had no cause for complaint at the result of their shot.

Caught in the blast from the two exploding cases, consternation and pandemonium reigned among the *Kweharehnuh*. Horses squealed, reared and a couple went down as musket balls struck them. The charge was halted and changed into a milling, plunging mass of men and horses.

Urged on by the gunners, the three howitzer crews made fast time in reloading and altering their aim. Before the amazed Indians could regain control of their startled horses, the next solid shot plunged down among them. Struck by the cannon ball, one of the *tehnap*'s heads dissolved into bloody pulp and the man next to him also went down. Then the two spherical case shells arrived. More men and horses went down under the hail of flying lead.

Brave warriors as the *Kweharehnuh* might be under normal circumstances, they had never faced cannon fire. Before the braves could recover, the well-served howitzers belched their third loads into the air. Taken with the sight of Goodnight leading his men at a charge along the river's bank, the arrival of the ball and two spherical cases proved to be the final straw. Only one of the cases exploded, but a ball from it caught the war-bonnet chief between the eyes and tumbled him from his horse.

Seeing their leader go down was all the rest of the demoralized band needed. Frightened of the unknown they might be, but they still scooped up all their wounded and most of the dead in the mad melee caused by turning to escape.

In the lead of his party, Goodnight saw that the decision to bring the howitzers along had been fully justified. Around three hundred *Kweharehnuh* had gathered, a force against which the cowhands and cavalrymen would have stood no chance in an open fight. Goodnight had hoped that the guns would produce panic, but knowing the nature of the enemy could not rely on it happening.

At the sight of their companions disrupted and broken by the artillery bombardment, without being aware of what caused it, the warriors at the mouth of the cave turned and ran. Not all them escaped, for the cowhands and soldiers cut loose with their revolvers on coming into shooting range. The rout, however, was as complete as it could be.

Charging his roan through the water, Goodnight galloped it to the mouth of the cave. He left the saddle with the horse still running, hurdled the bodies before the entrance and plunged inside with a Colt in his right hand. Cold anxiety bit into the rancher at what he saw. Loving sprawled against the rear wall, blood oozing from the bullet hole in his chest and welling up around the arrow which protruded from his body.

.The rescue had come just too late to prevent the trailblazing cattleman from being seriously wounded.

THREE

Those Texas Trail Hands Are
All Rebels

"How'd it go, John?" Goodnight asked his segundo, wanting to take his mind off what was happening in the cave.

"No trouble, Colonel," Poe answered. "Fact being, we handled the herd as easy, if not easier, than with the full crew."

Although Goodnight would remember the words at a later date, at that moment he gave them little attention. Rowdy Lincoln, the trail drive's cook, appeared at the entrance to the cave and approached the rancher. The cook's normally jovial features held an expression of worry and concern.

"I've got the bullet and arrow out, Colonel Charlie," Lincoln said, his voice easy and gentle as it was except on rare occasions. "But he's still in a mighty poor shape."

"Can we move him?" Goodnight inquired.

"His chances aren't good whether we take him with us, or let him rest up here. Maybe the post surgeon at Fort Sumner can do something when we get there—if Oliver lasts that long."

It was late afternoon on the day of the rescue and Rowdy Lincoln had just finished performing his secondary but equally important, function as part of the trail crew. Over the years, through force of necessity, the cook had gained much experience in the treatment of injuries received far from any qualified medical attention.

From the rim above the men came the sounds of the herd passing and John Poe had come down to learn how Loving fared. From all appearances, the cattleman was in a very bad way and it would tax Lincoln's considerable skill to keep him alive. However, Poe did not allow himself to fall into despondency.

"I'll get back to the herd, boss," Poe said quietly.

"Sure, John," Goodnight confirmed. "Look for a way down farther along. Water them, push across and find a bed-ground."

After a scouting party had been sent out and returned to say that the Comanches had left the area, Major Lane had made his preparations to continue the journey to Fort Sumner. He had, however, left half of his cavalry escort under a sergeant to travel with the herd and help fight off further Indian attacks.

Returning to the herd, Poe guided it along the rim, found an easy place to descend and completed his employer's orders. With the cattle bedded down on the western bank of the Pecos, the bed wagon was fitted out to carry the wounded Loving the remainder of the journey.

During the days which followed, Goodnight had many misgivings over his partner's welfare. The bed wagon was not designed for the transportation of a seriously wounded man. Yet Loving's chances would have been no greater if he had been left under a heavy guard at the cave. The cattleman's condition did not improve or seem to grow worse. Most of the time he lay in a condition of semicoma, never complaining, aware that his only slender hope was in reaching the post hospital at Fort Sumner.

Four days' drive—around forty miles—out of the Fort, Goodnight found that Major Lane had not forgotten Loving, an Army surgeon arrived with a Rocker Ambulance and small cavalry escort. Examining the wounded cattleman, the surgeon confirmed Rowdy's views, praised the cook's handling of the injuries and stated that only his skill had kept Loving alive. However, the cattleman's condition was critical and the surgeon wanted to deliver him to Fort Sumner as quickly as possible. The Rocker ambulance had been designed for the rapid transportation of wounded passengers over rough, roadless country and was the best vehicle of its kind so far.*

With Loving carried off in the Rocker ambulance, the trail drive continued. It went by smoothly, with no further incidents to mar its progress and the crew began to look forward to the pleasures awaiting them when they received their pay. For Goodnight, thoughts of his partner's condition lessened the pleasure he felt at having almost completed the drive and being one

*For a description of a Rocker Ambulance, read *Hound Dog Man*.

step closer to turning his dream into a practical reality.

The arrival of the herd created a stir of interest at the Fort and among the citizens of the small town which had grown up outside the walls of the Army post. Views on the matter in the latter area differed. Some considered that the Government should not waste money feeding "them stinking red varmints." Others, having a greater experience of matters Apache felt only relief that the Army would be able to keep its promises by supplying meat to the reservations.

However, interested as they were in the herd's arrival, the two men standing slightly away from the crowd of loafers outside the Yellow Stripe saloon subscribed to neither of the popular views. Their clothing showed that they did not belong to the area. Although travel-stained, their city suits were costly and well tailored. The heavy gold watch chains across their vests and other signs pointed at wealth beyond that of the general run of the onlookers and their sun-reddened features hinted they had recently come from some cooler climate to the heat-baked Territory of New Mexico. One was tall, bluff of appearance, with side-whiskers and a mouth which smiled frequently even though his eyes did not. More sober in selection of clothing and some six inches shorter than his companion, the other had a clean-shaven, sharp face with a thin, tight mouth.

"He made it, Joe," the bigger man remarked unnecessarily as they watched the herd being brought to a halt on the open ground to the west of the Fort.

"Yes, damn him. He made it," agreed the other. "Which doesn't mean that he'll get that Army beef contract."

"No. But they'll be more willing to consider him now he's brought in a herd."

"Maybe we should give them other things to consider about him coming here, Stu," the smaller of the dudes remarked. "Like reminding them how those Texas trail hands are all rebels. There'll be folks in this town who won't take kind to that."

With the herd brought to a halt, Goodnight looked to where the Army's cattle-buying commission were coming from the Fort. Led by Colonel Hunter, a tall, plump member of the Quartermaster Corps, the two majors and half-a-dozen enlisted men studied the cattle. Before he did anything else, Goodnight inquired as to his partner's condition and learned there was no change. Then the men got down to business. The price offered and accepted was one which Goodnight felt to be most satisfactory and of the greatest use to his future plans.

"We'll have to grade and examine the herd, of course," Hunter said, sounding almost apologetic and offering Goodnight a cigar from the number he carried in his jacket pocket. "It's not that I doubt your honesty, but you understand my position."

"I do," Goodnight assured him. "How about the weights?"

"Between us, we ought to reach a fair figure," the officer replied. "Shall we make a start, Mr. Goodnight?"

"Tell us what you want doing and we'll get it done," Goodnight answered.

"Can your men bring them up one at a time so that we can check their weight, condition and number?" Hunter requested. "It has to be done."

Low groans greeted the news of Goodnight's intentions. Most of the cowhands had expected to hand the cattle straight over to the soldiers and be left free to sample whatever delights or pleasures the town had to offer. Instead they found themselves sent to cut out every individual steer and lead it up for inspection by the buying commission. It promised to be a long, tedious, boring and possibly dangerous business.

First the captured steers were led by where John Poe, one of the majors and two corporals waited to count them. While the major's military assistants each held a tally book and pencil, the segundo kept his count with no greater aid than tying a knot in a length of cord for every hundredth steer to go by.

From being counted, each steer was taken to the second major. A qualified veterinary surgeon, he had to check the animal's condition; no easy matter despite the controlling rope about its neck. Fortunately few of the herd required a close inspection, being in excellent condition.

For all his excellently cut uniform under a knee-long white linen-duster jacket, air of pompous dignity and an almost political desire to keep everybody contented, Hunter rapidly proved himself a better than fair judge of cattle. He certainly knew sufficient to avoid falling into a basic error often made where Texas longhorn cattle were concerned.

Seeing a longhorn from the side for the first time, an inexperienced person might easily form a greatly exaggerated estimation of its poundage. Tall, leggy, flat-ribbed, a longhorn's profile produced an illusion of extra bulk and heft. Viewed from the rear, the cat hams, narrow hips and swayed, ridge-pole kind of backbone with a thin, high shoulder top dispelled such notions of excessive weight. As shown by the way the body tucked up in the flanks, or legs had length rather than bulky thickness, the longhorn's free-ranging way of life prevented it from being a quick converter of forage into beef and producing clean, heavy cuts of meat down to the hock. Any fat gathered in times of good grazing was disposed evenly about the body, instead of being stored in the belly or on the legs. Coarse of head and hair, carrying a great spread of needle-pointed horns, the Texas longhorn could run, jump, fight and live off the land in a manner which no carefully raised Eastern beef breed might hope to equal.

Clearly Hunter knew of the Longhorn's physical conformation. If his estimation of a given steer's weight tended to go under rather than over, it always came close enough to satisfy Goodnight. Between them, they were forming a fairly accurate total of the herd's poundage "on the hoof." While the price would have been at least double for dressed, butchered beef, the subsequent wastage of bone and hide had to be taken into consideration.

As might be expected, an audience soon formed. Loafers and other townfolk mingled with off-duty soldiers and hovered in the background to see what was going on. Among them were the two dudes who had commented so cryptically from the sidewalk outside the Yellow Stripe saloon about Goodnight's arrival.

"If that's all the weighing they get—" the bigger man began.

"It's got possibilities," agreed his companion.

At first the crowd saw nothing out of the ordinary, other than fine but normal riding and roping. The Texans worked fast and the sizes of the two bunches began to grow more even. Suddenly a big steer broke from the Army herd in a determined attempt to return and find its traveling companion with the unchecked cattle. Cut off by a fast-riding, tall, young cowhand the steer reversed its direction and headed toward the onlookers.

"Stop it!" roared the veterinarian, a man of hasty temper and conscious of his superiority over the less well-educated cowhands.

Already the young Texan had twirled his mount around and given chase. His rope hung coiled on his saddlehorn. There would be no time to free it, work open a loop and rope the fleeing red steer before it plunged in among the crowd. However, he knew how to handle the situation. That there was an appreciative audience, including several pretty girls, did nothing to lessen his intention of doing so.

The trained horse knew what was expected of it. Extending its stride, it crowded closer to the fleeing steer. The more nervous members of the crowd started to scatter before the menace of the long, spike-sharp horns and mean-looking heft of the big animal. Coming alongside it, the cowhand leaned across and grabbed its tail. A touch of his heels caused the horse to step aside and add its weight to the pull he gave at the tail. Thrown off balance, the steer went crashing to the ground. It bounced on landing, sliding to a halt before it reached the places so rapidly vacated by the front members of the crowd.

"Damn it!" the veterinarian bawled, starting toward the cowhand who slid his horse to a halt facing the steer. "Don't break the beast's neck!"

Annoyance flushed the young Texan's face. After performing a mighty neat "tailing down," he could see several of the female audience eyeing him in frank admiration and did not care to have the feeling spoiled by any damned shiny-butt, desk-warming Yankee.

"Go to hell!" the cowhand yelled back over his shoulder. "What should I've done, let it run all over some of these good folks here?"

"Get it shoved back with the others, Austin!" Goodnight barked, knowing the youngster to be high spirited and hot tempered. "The sooner we're through, the quicker you boys get your pay."

"Is that steer all right, Major?" Hunter went on, indicating a perfectly healthy animal being drawn up for inspection.

The words caused the tension to stop for the time being. Although the major's neck showed red above his collar, he swung back to his work. Snorting and grunting, the winded red steer lurched to its feet and stood shaking its head in a dazed manner. However, one good tailing had taught it a lesson and it lumbered quietly enough back to the herd.

Other steers continued to be passed between the examination teams. Cowhands changed their horses, grabbed a cup of coffee prepared by Rowdy Lincoln and his louse, the tall, gangling, excitable Turkey Trott. The latter also delivered coffee to the buying commission, allowing the work to continue unchecked. However, the veterinarian was still smarting under the sting of Austin's retort and apparent rebuke by Hunter. So he gave the cattle a closer scrutiny, which slowed down the proceedings. Wanting to check a *grulla** steer brought up by a sweating, tired Spat, the veterinarian acted rashly. Instead of warning the cowhand, he walked toward the *grulla*. It let out a low, warning snort that a more experienced man would have recognized, dropped its head and lunged forward. Wise to the ways of ropes, the steer had not fought against the pull. So the rope hung sufficiently slack for it to have the means of reaching the rash soldier. Even as the major threw himself to the rear, Spat made his horse jump sideways. Snapping tight, the rope jerked the steer to a halt. For all that, its wicked horns only

*Grulla: mousy brown color like the plumage of a sandhill crane.

missed the major by a couple of inches as its head hooked up in a belly-ripping slash.

Unable to stop himself, the major sat down hard. Hearing the laughter of the crowd increased his feeling of humiliation. Thrusting himself to his feet, he looked for someone on whom to vent his anger. The closest person, and most logical, was the lanky Spat.

"Why in hell don't you watch what you're doing, you damned beef-head?" yelped the veterinarian.

Normally Spat had an amiable nature, but he was feeling the strain of the long drive and the emotional stress of having left Loving and Sid to face the Indians. Nobody blamed him for the latter, there had been no other decision but for him to try and fetch help. However, Spat still felt that he might have been more use staying at the cave, even though he knew at the bottom of his heart that he had acted for the best. It all combined to make Spat most unappreciative of the soldier's comments.

"Watch what you're doing yourself, blue-belly!" he growled back, answering the major's derogatory name for a Texan with one equally opprobrious to the U.S. Army. "A kid in its cradle back home'd know better than *walk* up to a longhorn."

"Don't speak to a m—!" the major bellowed, thrusting himself erect.

"Get on with it, Major!" Hunter barked. "Nobody got hurt."

Watching the officer stalk angrily back to his original position, the two dudes exchanged knowing nods.

"With hotheads like those two cowboys, we ought to get something stirred up easy enough," commented the smaller man.

"That major'll be worth cultivating too," the other

replied. "He'll be on the board which awards the contract. What happens if Goodnight should get it, Joe?"

"We'll just have to make sure that he doesn't fulfill it," the smaller man stated. "It's as easy as that."

At last, with the sun going down, the last of the steers had passed before the buying commission and been accepted. Coming across, the veterinarian faced Goodnight and Hunter stiffly but did not allow personal feelings to interfere with his duty.

"They're all healthy and in good condition, Colonel."

"Thank you, sir," Goodnight answered.

Without making any reply, the veterinarian saluted Hunter, made a smart about-face and walked away.

"He'll calm down soon enough," Hunter told Goodnight, then looked at John Poe and the second major as they approached.

"I make the tally one thousand, five hundred and fourteen," the major announced, holding the two books in which his assistants had kept their count.

"And me," agreed Poe, still holding the length of pigging thong which had served him instead of pencil and paper. "Fifteen hundred and fourteen, just like on our last trail count,* boss."

"All branded with the Swinging G," the major went on.

"You was expecting maybe something else, soldier?" Poe inquired sardonically, having been aware how the major had studied the "G" brand burned on the left flank of each steer.

"I've my duty to do," the major replied stiffly.

"Have a cigar, Mr. Poe," Hunter put in hastily, producing a handful from his tunic pocket. "Take

---

*A trail count is described fully in *Trail Boss*.

some for the rest of your men."

"*Gracias,* Colonel," Poe answered and grinned at the major. "I know you don't want to buy stolen stock, friend. But was I you, I'd put that report a mite different next time you make it. Some folks'd be touchy about how it sounded."

"It wasn't a good choice of words, I'll admit," the major said and grinned back as Poe offered him one of the cigars, accepting it in terms of an olive branch. "You've done well to get that many here and in such good shape."

Although Poe knew Goodnight's thoughts on the subject, he did not comment on them. However, he felt that the major would be considerably surprised when the rancher declared his views at the contract meeting the following day.

"If you show us where you want 'em, we'll bed the herd down," Goodnight told Hunter, seeing harmony restored. "How about handling them?"

"I've two dozen troopers who've been cowhands for that," Hunter assured him. "You and your men can take a well-earned rest."

"Yahoo!" Austin whooped, having been close enough to hear the words. "It's not *resting* I'm fixing to do."

"You spook that herd and I know what you'll be doing!" Poe growled.

"They'll not spoke easy if you put them on good grazing and water," Goodnight remarked to Hunter.

"Good. If you'll accompany me to the Fort, I'll attend to your payment."

"I'll need some of it to pay off my crew," Goodnight admitted. "And John, I know the boys figure to drink the town dry. But make sure they remember that the War's over and I don't want it starting again."

FOUR

Who Did You Fight For In The War?

When the soldiers took charge of the bedded-down cattle, the trail crew headed for town at a gallop. Thundering along the main—and only—street, they brought their horses to a halt outside the Yellow Stripe saloon. Inside its doors, Goodnight was waiting with money to pay off his crew.

"What's this stuff, anyways?" Austin whooped, accepting his pay. "Is it what my pappy calls cash money and used to talk about afore mammy stopped him?"

"It for sure is," Spat agreed, jingling coins in his hands. "Least, I reckon it is. That gent behind the bar there'll likely tell us for sure."

Goodnight led the way to the bar on completing the

pay-out. Handing money across the counter, he called for drinks on the house. That brought a rush of customers as townsmen and soldiers gathered to accept the rancher's bounty. Among them were the Artillery sergeant major and the Cavalry sergeant who had stayed behind as escort for the herd during the latter stages of the journey, and some of their men who had enjoyed Texas hospitality on the trail.

"Man, I needed that!" young Austin whooped, upending four fingers of whisky and smacking his lips appreciatively. "Same again, barkeep, and for the *senorita* here."

Having expected a roaring night's trade, the owner of the saloon had brought in a number of pretty Mexican girls from the local cathouses. One of them stood at Austin's elbow, giggling her delight as he hugged her.

"Not for me right now," Goodnight replied when the youngster offered him a drink. "I'm going to see Oliver."

"Sure hope he's all right," Austin said seriously. "Of all the stinking—"

"He wouldn't want you boys thinking sorrowful about him," Goodnight pointed out. "Have some fun tonight, you've earned it, all of you." With that he turned to where Poe stood talking to the two noncoms. "John, see the boys have fun, but hold it down if they get too rowdy."

"I'll see to it," the segundo promised.

Leaving the saloon, Goodnight took his horse and rode out to the Fort. There he visited the hospital and learned that Loving's condition remained the same. Seeing his partner's unconscious face, pale and wracked with pain, Goodnight felt deeply concerned. However, the rancher wanted to return to his men.

Being aware of how easily the flames of Civil War hatred could rise, he wished to prevent any trouble starting between his men and the locals on that score. He knew his presence would be a big inducement to holding tempers in check.

Approaching the saloon, Goodnight heard singing. It rang out with gusto and gave every evidence of its maker's high spirits. For all that, the rancher felt a touch worried as he made out the words.

> *Lo, the beacon fires are lighted!*
> *Let all true hearts now stand united!*
> *To arms! To arms! To arms in Dixie!*

Swinging from his horse, the rancher tossed its reins over the hitching rail and strode swiftly toward the saloon's batwing doors. With the second verse of General Samuel Pike, the C.S.A.'s highly patriotic lyrics to Emmett's *Dixie* blaring out in full-throated chorus, he figured that he had better intervene and divert the singers to a less explosive choice of music. Even as he reached out a hand to open the door, the thing he feared happened.

Lurching from a table at the side of the barroom, a big, burly, unshaven man came to a halt in the center of the floor. He wore dirty range clothing, a filthy Burnside campaign hat and a U.S. Cavalry weapon belt with a revolver in its high-riding twist-hand draw holster.

"Stop that damned row!" the man bawled. "I'm not having any lousy rebel song sung here."

Instantly the atmosphere of genial enjoyment faded and the singing died away. The soldiers present eyed the cowhands in a speculative manner. Bringing their song to a halt, the Texans studied the burly objector. Austin took his arm from around the waist of the pretty Mexican girl and moved forward lifting his right hand until it hovered over the butt of his Colt.

"You're not, huh?" the youngster purred.

"The hell I am!" spat the burly man, a typical range-town loafer, or Goodnight had never seen the breed. "We licked you rebs once and—"

Knowing that something must be done, and done fast, Goodnight prepared to enter. However, he saw the Artillery sergeant major step from Poe's side and ask, "Who'd you fight for in the War, feller?"

"Huh?" grunted the big man, clearly not having expected the question "Why I fought for the Union, same's all these other gents."

Across the room, the group of men indicated by the Union-supporter muttered their agreement. They were of the same general social class as Herb Crutch and their sole claim to the title "gents" came from being his cronies. Cautious by nature, they waited to see the run of general public opinion before taking a definite stand on the issue. It seemed that the soldiers present did not give their unquestioned support to Crutch.

"I mean what outfit did *you* lick the rebs with?" the sergeant major clarified, ignoring everybody but Crutch.

The burly man seemed disinclined to answer. However, the information was not long in coming. Having taken in more money so far that evening than in any previous full-night's business, the bartender had no desire to kill off the golden goose. Nor had he any great liking for Crutch, whose custom rarely extended beyond buying a beer, in return for which he delved deeply in the free-lunch counter.

"He never served in no outfit, Sarge. Fact being, he spent the whole War out here hoss-catching for the Army."

Which was just about what the sergeant major figured. He had noticed before how men of Crutch's kind became vocal about dealing with the enemy but generally avoided taking any risks while doing it.

"Then bill out, stop-at-home!" growled the sergeant major.

"Yeah," agreed the cavalry sergeant, ranging himself alongside the other noncom. "I'm gut-full of fellers who sat on their butts at home, picking their noses all through the shooting, trying to keep the War going."

"And me," the sergeant major continued. "Only the stupid sons-of-a-bitch who want the War to go on didn't fight in it. And I never saw you hanging back when one of these Texas gents called up drinks for the house."

"Nor m—!" Austin began.

A big hand clamped hold of his arm, crushing it and he swung his head to look into the coldly warning face of Rowdy Lincoln.

"Leave be," ordered the cook. "Those gents're doing it right. Colonel Charlie says he wants things peaceable and peaceable they're going to stay."

Austin was smart enough to know when to listen. Not only did Rowdy have muscles to back his demands, but his position as cook gave him the means of wreaking a suitable revenge on anybody who crossed him. So Austin returned to the waiting girl.

Scowling around, Crutch saw no support to his stand for the glory of the Union. Even his special cronies showed reluctance to back his play. Taking their cue from the two noncoms, the soldiers refused to be sucked into attempts at restarting the Civil War. For the most part, the town-dwellers present did not care for the hulking, idle Crutch and saw no reason to antagonize a potential source of revenue on his behalf. Finding himself deserted by all, Crutch knew better than try to take the matter further. With a snarled-out, inaudible blanket curse, he turned and slouched toward the main doors. Seeing Goodnight just entering the saloon, Crutch's surly temper led him into recklessness.

"Get the hell out of my way, beef-head!" Crutch snarled.

Which, as any of the Swinging G trail crew could have warned him, was no way to address Colonel Charlie Goodnight. Maybe the rancher desired a peaceable evening; but there were limits to how far he would go to achieve his desire. Let a man of that kind get away with such behavior and he would try further abuses. So Goodnight continued to walk forward.

"I'm going across to the bar, *hombre*," the rancher said calmly and without bluster, meeting the other's threatening gaze, "and I'm too tired to walk round you."

There Crutch had it. His challenge had been taken up and countered. Sensing that every eye in the saloon was on him, he knew he must try to make some play, or get out of Fort Sumner as a braggart who failed to back up his words.

Something about Goodnight's stocky, powerful frame warned Crutch against attempting a physical assault. Which left only one other course open. Letting out a menacing snarl, the loafer reached toward his holster—and learned a basic, but deadly dangerous fault in its construction. To take out his revolver, he had first to open the holster's flap. The same did not apply to Goodnight. Dropping his right hand, the stocky rancher gripped and raised the waiting Colt from leather.

Shock licked into the burly man as he found himself looking at the .44 bore of Goodnight's Army Colt. He realized that, despite making the first move, he was far, far too slow. Nor would anybody present blame the rancher if he let the hammer fall.

Goodnight was no trigger-wild killer with a yen to see victims kicking at his feet. Instead of shooting, he waited until the frightened man's hand dropped away from the holster flap, lowered his Colt's hammer to the safety notch between two of the cylinder's chambers and returned the weapon to leather.

"I'm still going to the bar," the rancher announced flatly. "And I'm still too tired to walk around you."

Crutch moved hurriedly aside. Without even another glance at the man, Goodnight continued his leisurely stroll in the direction of the bar. Although a spectacular-appearing act, the rancher knew it to be comparatively safe. With so many men watching him, Crutch would be unlikely to take the chance offered by Goodnight's back. Nor did he. Moving with considerably more than usual speed, the loafer passed through the batwing doors and into the night.

The sergeant major let out a low sigh of relief, then nodded to a tall, swarthy, black haired member of his Battery. Finishing his drink, the soldier made for a side door and went out. If Goodnight noticed the Incident, he made no mention of it. Instead he made a start at relieving the tension which he sensed still hovered in the background.

"We've had *Dixie*," the rancher told his men. "Now let's have *Yankee-Doodle*, shall we?"

Led by John Poe and Rowdy Lincoln, the Texans roared out a lusty—if not over-musical—response to their boss's request. Even Austin joined in. With the cook's coldly menacing eyes on him, he could do nothing else. Their spirited rendering of *Yankee-Doodle* worked and the supporters of the Union accepted it in the right spirit. After which a good evening's fun was had by all.

Goodnight was clean, tidy and barbered next morning when he went to face the Army's cattle-buying commission. Nor did his face show the deep worry he felt over his partner's worsened condition. Much as he had wanted to stay at the hospital in case Loving recovered from the coma, Goodnight had forced himself to attend the meeting.

On entering the room, he found General Vindfallet—commanding the New Mexico Territory army posts—Colonel Hunter, the Fort's commanding officer and the two majors from the previous day seated at a table. In the room also were two civilians whom Goodnight remembered having seen watching the herd's arrival.

"I'm sorry I'm late, gentlemen," Goodnight greeted.

"We understand," Vindfallet replied. "May I say how sorry we all are to hear of your partner's decline."

"This's Mr. Wednesbury and Mr. Hayden of the Mutual Land & Cattle Company," Hunter introduced, indicating first the taller then the second dude, who nodded their response. "Now, gentlemen, shall we get down to business?"

"That's why we're here," Vindfallet answered.

Hunter told of the Army's future requirements. With some eleven thousand Indians on the New Mexico reservations to be fed, considerable numbers of cattle would be needed and the Government was willing to pay well to fill their requirements. Watching his competitors, Goodnight saw their faces register slight annoyance on hearing that only steers would be bought. He knew that the Army had made a wise decision and one beneficial to the Texas cattle industry. Hunter's mention of the price the Army would pay drove all such thoughts from Goodnight's head. Long schooled in poker-playing and dealing with Indians who could read correctly the slightest facial expression, Goodnight needed all his skill to prevent his interest showing.

"That's a fair price," Hayden remarked.

"It's a damned fine price," Vindfallet put in. "How about it, can you fill our needs?"

"Of course," Wednesbury stated.

"I can," Goodnight went on.

"Will your partner be recovered sufficiently to do so?" Hayden asked. "We've all heard of Oliver Loving's ability in handling cattle; it is matched only by your ability as a scout."

"What you're trying to say," Goodnight answered calmly, "is can I handle the drives without Oliver. I hope I don't have to; but if the need arises, I can. I know the trail as well as any man and have had sufficient experience with cattle to handle them. Have you gentlemen similar knowledge?"

"Our trail managers have. They worked with Jubal Early during the War."

"Didn't you have some trouble last night, Mr. Goodnight?" Hayden continued when Wednesbury stopped talking.

"Not that I know of," the rancher answered.

"You had to draw a gun on a man."

"That was no trouble."

"The man was objecting to your men singing *Dixie*," Hayden said.

"That wasn't why I drew on him," Goodnight corrected. "The incident was over, ended by two noncoms from the Fort, before he tried to pull a gun on me. I did no more than necessary to stop him shooting me."

"We've heard of the incident, Mr. Hayden," Hunter injected.

"To save further questioning on that line," Goodnight went on. "I rode with Captain Cureton's Rangers throughout the War."

Nods of approval came from the listening soldiers. The fame of Cureton's Rangers had extended beyond the borders of Texas. Without their handling of the Indian situation, both the Union and Confederacy would have faced considerable difficulties with the various hostile tribes.

"The War is over, gentlemen," Vindfallet put in. "Right now, our concern is not with who fought on which side, but arranging to supply beef for the Government. And deciding whether you can deliver it to us."

"We can," Hayden declared firmly.

"So can I—" Goodnight began.

"We'll have fifteen hundred head here by the end of July." Wednesbury interrupted. "All steers. And can follow them up at regular intervals as needed."

"Will you have sufficient cattle to keep up a supply, Mr. Goodnight?" Hunter inquired.

"In addition to my own ranch, I've an arrangement with John Chisum to fill my needs," Gooodnight answered.

There was a knock on the door and a young lieutenant looked inside.

"Could Mr. Goodnight step outside for a moment, sir?" he asked.

"Excuse me, gentlemen," Goodnight said, standing up.

After the rancher had left the room, Hayden

coughed, then said, "Our men will be selected, not a pack of roughnecks."

"I haven't heard any complaints against Goodnight's crew." Hunter pointed out. "They were rowdy, but did no damage that wasn't more than amply paid for."

"They're rebs—" the veterinarian put in, still smarting as he thought of how two of them had addressed him.

"They're civilians," Hunter corrected. "You can't bawl them out and expect them to take it like buck-privates."

"I'd say the matter is not the behavior of the men when they get here," Vindfallet put in, "but whether they can bring the cattle in. The civil authorities can deal with how they behave on arrival."

Hearing the low mutter of approval from the commission, Wednesbury and Hayden knew their first line of defense had collapsed.

With a sinking heart, Goodnight walked over to where the post surgeon was waiting. The rancher knew what message the other brought, even before the doctor told him that Loving had died.

"How was it?" Goodnight asked.

"He was in no pain. In fact he recovered consciousness just before he died. He asked me to tell you something—"

"Yes—?"

"He said, 'Make your dream come true, Charlie,'" the doctor answered.

"Thank you, Doctor," Goodnight said.

"Are you all right?" the doctor inquired.

"I'll be all right," the rancher replied and turned to walk slowly back in the direction of the room from which he had come.

Thoughts churned at Goodnight as he approached the door. However, as he opened it, he reached his decision. It was the one to be expected from Charles Goodnight—whom the Comanches called Dangerous Man—and which he knew his dead partner would have approved of. While his scheme might sound wild and impractical, he felt certain that he could carry it out. So, although nothing showed on his face, he was seething with excitement as he returned to the commission.

"If you want, we'll cancel the meeting until tomorrow," Vindfallet offered on learning of Loving's death.

"No," Goodnight answered.

"These gentlemen have offered to deliver fifteen hundred head to us by the end of July, Mr. Goodnight," Hunter said. "What do you say to that?"

"I'll have three thousand head here, by the first week in July," Goodnight replied. "And I'll put up any sum of money you ask for as bond against my doing so."

Half an hour later, Hayden and Wednesbury entered their room at the hotel. Hurling his hat angrily on to the bed, the bigger man let out a savage curse.

"So Goodnight got the contract, Stu," Hayden said philosophically. "It could be good for us."

"How's that?"

"When he can't make it, none of those other beef-head bastards will try."

"Where do we stop him? Here, before he leaves," asked Wednesbury.

"No thanks!" Hayden snorted. "We're going to use better men than that lard-gutted Crutch you paid to stir up trouble."

"How was I to know some damned blue-belly'd take the Texan's side in it?" Wednesbury protested. "At least Crutch had the sense not to come back here."

"That's about all he did right. He didn't start trouble with the Texans, or scare the cattle so that they ran and were lost."

"Maybe something stopped him from doing it," Wednesbury said.

Only the word should have been "somebody," not "something." In return for their part in giving him a booster for arrival to Fort Sumner, Major Lane had told his sergeant major to make sure the Texans received fair treatment and were not troubled by the local inhabitants. When Crutch had left the saloon, he was followed by "Gypsy" Smith of the Mountain Artillery Battery. At first the soldier had thought that Crutch intended to go home. When the man left town on foot, Smith followed and wondered what was taking him in the direction of the bedded-down cattle. Maybe Smith had never been a cowhand, but he knew enough about animals to figure what would happen if somebody started firing off a revolver close to the sleeping longhorns. Seeing Crutch draw his weapon, Smith had moved fast.

Feeling the clip-point of a Green River blade prodding at his back, Crutch forgot his idea of stampeding the herd and laying the blame on a drunken Texas cowhand working off spite against the Yankees. He was aware, even without Smith's comments on the matter, of his fate if news of the attempt became public. Being a realist, he knew his social standing to be low around Fort Sumner. Several people would be only too pleased to see him run out, if nothing worse. So, on being dismissed by the soldier, he had wasted no time in gathering his few belongings and taking his departure without visiting the two men who had made him such tempting offers for his assistance in stirring feelings against the Texans.

"Come morning we'll head for Throckmorton," Hayden decided after a brief discussion. "We'll be there in time to decide our next move."

"What's it likely to be?" Wednesbury wanted to know.

"Something better organized than anything we tried here," Hayden promised. "We'll make damned sure that he never gets here with that herd of cattle."

FIVE

You've Got Some Of My Cattle
In That Herd

"Now you're quite sure that you can manage all right, Charlie?" Mrs. Loving asked as she sat in the stagecoach waiting to leave the town of Graham, county seat of Young County, Texas. "If you can't, I'll—"

"I've all I need," Goodnight replied hurriedly. "I only wish that there was more I could do for you."

"You've done too much for me already," the woman smiled. "With forty thousand dollars, I can live comfortably in Austin."

The $40,000 represented Loving's full share of the partnership's money. Under different conditions, much of the profits would have gone to help with the fulfilment of Goodnight's dream. Knowing the precari-

ous nature of his scheme, the rancher could not ask
Mrs. Loving to risk losing everything by sharing in it.
Sure she would have agreed willingly, but Goodnight
wanted to see her settled with sufficient funds to
maintain her family. With that in mind, he planned to
stake everything he owned to make his dream come
true. If he failed, he had no dependants and could
easily start again.

With final condolences, Goodnight stood back and
allowed the stage to move off. The past was over and
done with. Down in front of the Demon Rum saloon
stood the future.

Tall, heavy set, bald, John Chisum leaned against
the hitching rail of the saloon and watched Goodnight
walk toward him. It would be several years before
Chisum attained his title of "The Cattle King" but he
dressed at the height of his fortunes in much the same
manner as he did while waiting for Goodnight—like a
saddle-bum. A cheap old woolsey hat was thrust back
on his hairless dome, while his cotton bandana,
hickory shirt, patched levis pants and scuff-heeled
boots were the cheapest money could buy. If he was
noticeable for anything, it was the fact that he did not
wear a gun, an unarmed man being something of a
novelty in Texas at that time. Most of the time his face
held an expression of disarming joviality. Apart from
his cold, shrewd eyes, he looked amiable and
completely trustworthy. Most folk failed to notice the
eyes until too late.

"Got her off all right, Charlie?" Chisum said.

"Yes," Goodnight answered shortly.

"Ain't nobody can say you didn't do right by her,"
Chisum commented. "Say, thanks for sending those
four boys out to hold the herd while my crew come to
town for a spell."

Although Goodnight had not sent his men to meet Chisum with that purpose in mind, he did not debate the point.

"Let's go out and look at the cattle, shall we?" Goodnight suggested.

"Well," Chisum answered in a hesitant manner, throwing a look to the saloon. "I was figuring on going in. The boys like to have ole Uncle John buy 'em a drink when they're in town."

"There'll be time for it," Goodnight stated.

"Shucks, the herd's held not half a mile out," Chisum said. "'Less you want to cut it right now, you can see it easy enough from the edge of town."

"I just want to make sure where it's held," Goodnight replied. "Let's go."

Neither of the ranchers noticed a rider coming along the street from the east, nor a man pointing them out to the newcomer. Walking in the opposite direction, they passed the building which housed the sheriff's office and jail. While making for the edge of town, Goodnight raised a point which puzzled him about the other's arrival.

"Pitzer moved fast to pick up eleven hundred head and bring them here already, John."

"He's a good boy and a fast worker," Chisum replied cheerfully, which was not how he had thought of his younger brother a couple of weeks earlier. "Cattle're easy enough to come by."

"Yeah," Goodnight agreed in a noncommittal tone.

"If your boys can handle them, they might's well take them out to your herd right off," Chisum suggested. "That'll give 'em all the time to get settled together afore we start the drive."

Goodnight looked across the open range to where a

large bunch of cattle were grazing under the care of his four men. He considered Chisum's words, knowing them to have wisdom. The more time the steers had to become acquainted with his own stock, the less trouble there would be when the drive to Fort Sumner started. From the noise inside the Demon Rum saloon, few of Chisum's hands would be ready to resume work that day. So his own men could either hold the herd where it was until morning, or ease it over to where the Swinging G's bunch were waiting to start the journey.

Although the men heard the sound of the approaching horse, neither gave it any attention. As Goodnight opened his mouth, something happened to prevent him speaking.

"You've got some of my cattle in that herd!'

Anger crackled in the voice which sounded from behind the two men. A girl was stabbing an accusing finger in the direction of the grazing cattle and glaring in a hostile manner at Chisum.

Tall, slender, with a figure fast ripening into full womanhood, the girl made an attractive picture seated astride a line-backed *bayo-tigre* gelding. Her blonde hair was tucked under a battered white Jeff Davis Confederate campaign hat, the brim of which threw a protective shadow on to her pretty, tanned face. She wore a short rawhide jacket over an open-necked blue shirt and levis pants hanging cowhand style with the cuffs outside her high-heeled riding boots. Around her waist hung a military-style weapon-belt with a Cooper Navy revolver butt forward in the open-topped holster at its right side.

At any other time Goodnight might have regarded the girl's choice of clothing with mingled disapproval at its lack of femininity and appreciation for its charm.

He slowly turned his eyes in Chisum's direction. Something in the bald rancher's manner gave Goodnight a hint of suspicion.

"How about it, John," asked Goodnight, "do you have any of this young lady's cattle with your herd?"

"Brother Pitzer's brought eleven hundred head at least, Charlie," Chisum answered, looking his most guileless. "You know I've not had time to look 'em over yet. Could be that maybe a couple or so of her'n's strayed in if the boys drove the herd across her land."

"A couple or so!" the girl spat out. "They run off a bunch of over a hundred that we'd gathered and were holding. Damn it! I saw them do it!"

Studying the girl's face, Goodnight doubted if the righteous indignation on it could be assumed to give strength to a lie. He knew that the incompetence of Chisum's younger brother had caused the loss of a large herd on its way to Young County. On receiving the news, Chisum had stated his intention of rectifying the situation. He ordered Pitzer to return and gather sufficient of his Long Rail or unbranded stock to replace the lost cattle. Despite the vast numbers of longhorns roaming the unfenced Texas ranges, Goodnight had been surprised when Pitzer returned so quickly. If the girl was telling the truth, the rapidity with which Chisum's brother had collected the replacement herd was explained.

One thing Goodnight knew for sure: the girl's allegation had to be investigated and prompt action taken if it were true.

"It's easy enough settled, John," Goodnight said. "You'll have the herd cut and the young lady can point out any of her brand that she sees. We'll need help to do it."

"Some of my boys're down to the Demon Rum

saloon," Chisum answered reluctantly, although only a man who knew him real well would have noticed the change in his voice.

Goodnight was such a man, so he said, "We'll go and fetch them."

"I'll come with you," the girl announced.

"To a saloon?" asked Goodnight.

"I'd go to a saloon, a hawg-ranch, or any other damned place to get those steers back!" the girl assured him hotly. "We'd gathered them to sell to a buyer and need the money they'll bring real bad."

"Come with us then," Goodnight offered. "You say that you saw the men who took the steers?"

"I sure as hell did. It was up in the Wallace Valley three days back. My hoss'd gone lame and I was headed for the house to get another when they come."

"You'd know the men if you saw them again then?"

"I sure will, Colonel Charlie."

"How come they let you see 'em?" asked Chisum. "Cow thieves ain't often so all-fired obliging."

"I got hid up among the black chaparral in a draw afore they saw me," the girl explained, directing her words mainly in Goodnight's direction. "Couldn't see who they was when I heard them coming, 'cepting we don't hire that many men, and a-foot I sure didn't figure to stand in plain sight to find out."

The girl, young as she was, knew how to act when alone on the range. Goodnight could see no reason for her to be lying about the theft, yet felt puzzled by at least one thing.

"How did you know who owned the cattle and who I am?"

"Feller back along the street told me who you was and pointed you out when I asked him about the herd. Which same's why I come here afore going to see the sheriff. My pappy's told me plenty about you, Colonel Charlie."

"Do I know him?"

"You likely do, Colonel. He's Darby Sutherland. My name's Dawn."

"Darby Sutherland, huh!" Goodnight grunted. "I know him."

"Why didn't your pappy come instead of sending you, gal?" Chisum inquired.

Clearly Dawn Sutherland's friendly feelings and trust did not extend to Chisum. She lost the smile and expression of pleasure which had crept to her face at Goodnight's words.

"'Cause he got stove up when a hoss threw him and isn't back on his feet yet. I'd've gone straight to see Sheriff Carlin, only I figured that Colonel Charlie'd do right by me."

"And I will," Goodnight promised. "Let's go and get your men, John."

"Sure," Chisum agreed, beaming in his most winning manner at Dawn. "I'm's keen as you are to get this straightened out."

If Dawn's expression was anything to go by, Chisum had failed by a good country mile to win her over. Swinging from her saddle, she walked at Goodnight's side with the *bayo-tigre* following her on loosely held reins. As he accompanied them along the street, Chisum tried to make light conversation but failed. While his face and voice remained placid and friendly, his eyes took on a wolf-cautious, almost menacing glint.

The Demon Rum saloon was doing remarkably good business considering that the day had advanced only a little beyond noon. Its band played in blaring opposition to laughter, shouts and a continuous hum of conversation. Outside, horses lined the hitching rails. Dawn secured her *bayo-tigre* gelding in the only place available, next to a big, shapely bloodbay stallion. Beyond it were two equally good animals, a paint as fine as the girl had ever seen and a magnificent white that looked as wild as a free-running mustang despite the low-horned, double-girthed saddle on its back.

Under different circumstances the girl would have spent time admiring the fine-looking horses and Goodnight might have found at least one of them of considerable interest had he noticed it. Wanting to regain possession of her father's cattle, Dawn contented herself with a swift glance while knotting her reins to the hitching rail. For a moment she wavered before the entrance. Since her earliest days, she had been taught that a 'good' woman did not enter saloons. Only for a moment, though. Then her purpose in coming to Graham overrode her prejudices. Setting her face grimly, she followed the ranchers through the batwing doors.

Once inside the barroom, Dawn found herself wishing that she had left the visit to Goodnight. Slowly the talk died down as every eye turned to the new arrivals. Dawn could sense the cold hostility of the garishly dressed women present and knew that they resented her invasion of their domain. However, in the company of two prominent members of the ranching community, she had little to fear from the saloon's female employees.

Naturally the appearance of a girl dressed as Dawn was could be calculated to attract attention. The cowhands speculated on why Colonel Charlie had allowed Dawn to accompany him inside. Being a gentleman in the strictest sense of the word, he would

not bring a young woman into a saloon as a joke or
merely to let her see what the inside of one looked like.

Seated at the left of the room, two men watched the
arrival and guessed at what it meant. The taller of the
pair wore all black clothing, from his Stetson hat,
through bandana, shirt, levis pants and down to his
boots. Even his gunbelt was of black leather, carrying a
walnut-handled Dragoon Colt butt forward in the
holster on its right side and an ivory hilted James Black
bowie knife sheathed at the left. Such an armament did
not go well with his apparent youth and Indian-dark,
almost babyishly innocent, handsome features. Yet a
closer examination of his eyes, red-hazel in color and
with a reckless, alien wildness glinting in them, would
have led one to believe that the weapons were anything
but an affectation.

Compared with his somberly dressed and somehow
dangerous-looking companion, the other man hardly
rated a second glance—on the surface. He would be at
most five-foot six in height, his dusty blond hair a
contrast with the raven-black locks of the dark
youngster. Good, regular features, but not eye-
catching in any way, held strength and inner power if
one cared to look. While the black Stetson, hanging
from the back of his chair, scarlet bandana, grey shirt,
levis pants and hand-made boots were expensive, he
contrived to make them look like somebody's castoffs.
They tended to hide the well-developed muscular
physique under them. A matched brace of bone-
handled 1860 Army Colts rode butt forward in
carefully designed cross-draw holsters.

"That's the gal we saw back on the Wallace, ain't it,
Dusty?" asked the dark young man, shoving back his
chair as if to rise.

"Sure looks like her," the small blond answered.

"Stay put a-whiles, Lon. I want to hear what's up first."

Coming to a halt in the center of the room, Goodnight looked around but failed to locate Pitzer Chisum. Nor did he know any of the men who had helped deliver the suspect herd.

"Get some of your crew over here, John," Goodnight commanded.

"Sure," Chisum answered. "They ain't all on hand, mind."

"We'll make do with them you can raise and my boys," Goodnight told him.

"Targue!" Chisum called. "Come on up here. Bring Keck, Venner and Alden with you. That's all of 'em who're here, Charlie."

"Looks like we called it right, Dusty," commented the dark youngster as four men rose from a table and made for Goodnight's party. "What'll we do?"

"Amble over quiet-like and listen to what's being said," his companion replied.

"Where's Pitzer?" Chisum asked his tall, lanky, hard-looking segundo.

"Him and most of the boys went down to Sadie's place," Targue answered. "They hea—"

"Them's the three who took my cattle!" Dawn ejaculated, pointing at Targue's companions.

SIX

I'm a Man And I'm Saying
You're a Liar!

Dressed in ordinary cowhand clothes, the trio indicated by Dawn had a hard and truculent air about them that did not entirely spring from their trail-dirty or unshaven condition. Army Colts hung from each's belt and none of them moved his right hand too far from from the gun's butt. Tallest of the three, Keck wore a wolfskin jacket. Venner was of middle height, a lean man with a sharp face and eyes that never stayed still. Although the shortest by a couple of inches, Alden held the advantage in weight. His surly, unintelligent features always held a scowl and he seemed perpetually on the lookout for somebody to attack.

"What's she yapping about?" demanded Keck.

"Allows you boys took off with a bunch of her folk's

cattle," Chisum replied, his face still bland and mild.

"And they did!" Dawn snapped.

"You saw them up this close?" Chisum asked.

Even the band had stopped playing and all sounds ended as the crowd listened to what they sensed might be the prelude to a dramatic situation. Even with conditions as they were in Texas, the theft of cattle was no light matter.

"Not from real close," Dawn admitted. "I was hid up in a draw maybe a hundred yards off when they rode in and took our cattle."

"She's *loco*, Uncle John," Keck announced. "We never took no damned herd."

"They did so take it!" Dawn yelled, excitement and anger making her incautious. "He's a liar!"

"You wouldn't be saying that if you wasn't a woman!" Keck snarled, face cold and ugly with menace.

"I'm a man and I'm saying you're a liar!" put in a quiet, drawling voice from the right of the party.

Slowly, exuding menace at every move, Targue and the other three Long Rail men turned to discover who dared intervene in such a manner. With fingers spread and hands poised ready to swoop on to their Colts' butts, they looked at the tall, dark youngster and his small, insignificant companion.

"Which of you said that?" Keck growled.

"Me," the dark youngster answered mildly. His eyes and bearing did not match the voice. Standing in a relaxed slouch, he managed to convey an air of latent, deadly readiness. All too casually his right hand trailed palm out close to the worn walnut grip of the heavy Dragoon Colt.

"Lon's right, though," the small Texan went on. "You are a liar."

In some way he seemed to have taken on size and heft, apparently growing in seconds to become a *big* man fully as dangerous as his dark-faced companion.

Throwing a glance at Chisum, Targue caught an almost imperceptible shake of the bald head. It conveyed a warning of danger which he read and accepted. So, he let his hand drop and edged away from the trio. Having failed to catch the rancher's signal, Keck and the other two tensed ready to take the appropriate action they felt would be expected of them.

Customers and employees around the room prepared to make hurried dives for cover. In frontier Texas, the word "liar" was never spoken lightly or as a joke. Its use, counted as a deadly insult and called for an answer from one of Colonel Colt's highly prized products.

"That's a hard way of putting things, young fellers," Chisum commented in a placating tone. "There's some *men* who don't take kind to being called a liar."

If Chisum intended to quieten down the hostility, he took a mighty poor way of doing it. Emphasizing the youth of the newcomers and pointing out the insult to the trio's manhood merely served to stiffen Keck, Venner and Alden to their intentions. So they showed no sign of being placated. Before any of them could speak, Goodnight injected a warning.

"Afore you start objecting, maybe you'd best know who's calling you a liar."

"And maybe we ain't caring who they are," Venner replied.

"Have it your way," Goodnight drawled and pointed first to the small Texan, then at his companion. "Only this here's my nephew, Dusty Fog, and I'd say this's the Ysabel Kid."

Sucking in his breath sharply, Keck moved his right hand from over the Colt's butt but let the left remain thumb-hooked on his waist-belt just under the right flap of his jacket. At the same time his companions allowed their truculent, menacing attitudes to sag away.

There were few people in Texas who had not heard of Dusty Fog. At seventeen, he had worn a captain's collar bars and led Company "C" of the Texas Light Cavalry on the highly successful raids which caused the Yankee Army of Arkansas so much damage and trouble. It had been Dusty Fog who helped Belle Boyd, the Rebel Spy, to buy a consignment of arms for the South with money looted from a Yankee paymaster* and in her company had smashed a gang of counterfeiters who planned to flood the Confederate States with their products.† Although few people knew of it, he had also foiled a plot by fanatical Union supporters to arm and send on the warpath the Indian tribes of Texas.* With the War over, Dusty had returned to his home in the Rio Hondo country. The crippling of his uncle, Ole Devil Hardin, had put him into the post of segundo on the great OD Connected ranch. Recently Dusty had been sent into Mexico on a mission of vital national importance and brought it to a successful conclusion.†

Small of stature Dusty Fog might be, but he already had a name for being lightning fast and very accurate in the use of his matched Colts. There were other stories told, of his uncanny skill at bare-hand fighting; how he knew methods to render bigger, stronger men helpless.

*Told in *The Colt and the Saber*.
†Told in *The Rebel Spy*.
*Told in *The Devil Gun*.
†Told in *The Ysabel Kid*.

No trio of hardcases would willingly go up against such a man; especially when he stood backed by the Ysabel Kid.

Born in the village of the *Pehnane* Comanche, the son of a wild Irish-Kentuckian horse-hunter and a Creole-Comanche girl, the Kid had been raised as a *Nemenuh* by his grandfather, Long Walker, who was chief of the Dog Soldier lodge.‡ By his fifteenth birthday, the boy had already earned his man-name among the *Pehnane*. They called him *Cuchilo*, the Knife, a tribute to his skill in using one. When his father adopted a new family business of smuggling across the Texas-Mexico border, the Kid had put his Indian-training to good use and gained a reputation as real bad medicine to cross. While not exceptionally fast with his old Dragoon, he could perform adequately with it and he took seconds to no man at wielding a knife or when tossing lead from a rifle.

Down along the Rio Grande, as a smuggler and while running shipments delivered through the blockading West Gulf Squadron of the Yankee Navy into Mexico the Kid built up a name likely to give pause to anybody figuring to make trouble for him. Nobody with a desire to stay alive and healthy voluntarily tangled with the Ysabel Kid.

"Why'd you say he's a liar, Kid?" asked Goodnight, when sure that the trio accepted his introduction.

"'Cause he's lying in his teeth when he says him and his pards didn't take off with the lady's stock," the dark youngster replied. "We saw 'em do it."

"Like Lon says, Uncle Charlie," Dusty went on. "We saw them. Didn't think much about it, though, until we saw the lady here come out of hiding."

"You could've rid over and said something right

‡Told in *Comanche*.

then, Cap'n Fog," Chisum put in. "It'd've saved all this unpleasantness."

"Have you been up the Wallace Valley way, Mr. Chisum?" Dusty asked without taking his attention from the trio.

"Can't say's I have," the rancher admitted.

"That figures," Dusty said coldly. "We were on the wrong side of a deep canyon and no way to get across it. So, time we'd rid around it the lady's cattle were already mixed in with your herd."

"I never saw you around," Targue commented.

"That's 'cause we didn't aim to let you," the Kid replied. "They do say's cow thieves're a mite touchy over letting folks look too close at their stock."

"I can't say's how I take to being called a cow thief!" Targue growled, being made of sterner, more dangerous stuff than the other three.

"Ease off there, Wally," counselled Chisum mildly. "Likely the Kid didn't mean it the way it sounded."

"Hell, Uncle John," Keck said, a light of inspiration flickering on his face. "It's all a mistake. We thought them cattle was strays."

"*Strays*!" Dawn snorted. "They're all branded plain enough to see."

"It's easy enough settled," Chisum stated, beaming at the girl like a martyr blessing the stone-throwers. "Keck, we'll go to the herd and cut out any of the lady's stock that we find."

Keck remarked, "I'll go. You boys stay on and buy these gents a drink to show there's no hard feelings."

"I'll buy the drinks," Chisum offered. "If the young lady doesn't mind us taking 'em in her company, that is."

"Go to it," Dawn answered. "All I want to do's get those steers back."

"What brings you out this way, Cap'n Fog?"

Chisum inquired, turning toward the bar as Keck walked across the room. "Did Ole Devil send you?"

"Sure," Dusty replied and he had once more shrunk to being the insignificant nobody he usually appeared.

Crossing the room, Keck took extra care to keep his right hand in plain sight. However, his left hand inched farther under the jacket until its fingers curled around the butt of the Metropolitan Navy Pocket revolver in its carefully designed, concealed holster. His every instinct gave warning of danger. In John Chisum's home town, there would have been little to fear from the girl's accusation. Unfortunately, Graham did not lie in an area where Chisum possessed influence over the local law. So Keck and his companions stood a better than fair chance of winding up in jail, if not suspended from a hang-rope, for their actions on the Wallace Valley.

A quick, surreptitious look over his shoulder told Keck that Chisum and Targue had moved out of the possible line of fire and he knew that his two companions were ready to back his play. Telling Alden and Venner to buy the drinks had alerted them to what he planned; they had used a similar method on another occasion. At the door, Keck would turn and start throwing lead with the Metropolitan. Even if he did not hit Dusty Fog or the Ysabel Kid, his bullets ought to take them by surprise and give his pards a chance to get into action.

Keck slipped the short-barreled revolver from beneath his jacket. Cocking back the hammer, he started to turn. Just an instant too late he heard the sound of somebody entering the barroom.

"Uncle Devil sent us along to help Uncle Charlie with this next drive he's making," Dusty continued in answer to Chisum's question.

"We've not met afore," Chisum remarked in a booming, jovial tone, as he moved toward the bar. "Maybe you've heard Ole Devil speak of me, John Chisum."

"I've heard," Dusty agreed but decided that it would not be polite to mention the manner in which Ole Devil Hardin invariably referred to the bald rancher's morals and business principles. "We'd have been here sooner, Unc—"

"Watch it, Dusty!" roared a voice from across by the main entrance.

Oblivious of the man who came into sight and entered the Demon Rum, Keck started to make his treacherous attack. Yet he could hardly have over-looked the newcomer if his mind had not been so fully occupied with the thoughts of escape.

A costly white Stetson with a silver concha-decorated band added to the new arrival's six-foot three inches of height, topping a great spread of shoulders that tapered down to a lean waist and long, powerful legs. From the tight-rolled green silk bandana which trailed its long ends down the front of a grey broadcloth shirt and the elegant cut of the levis pants hanging cowhand fashion free from the fancy-stitched boots, he was a wealthy young man and something of a dandy. About his middle swung a hand-stamped gunbelt of high-grade workmanship with two ivory-handled Army Colts in the contoured holsters, the butts flaring out a little for easy and rapid withdrawal. All in all, he made a fine figure. Golden blond hair framed a face of almost classically handsome lines, tanned, strong and intelligent.

Dandy the blond giant might be, but he showed a shrewd judgment of the situation and, despite his size, moved with considerable speed. Yelling a warning, he thrust through the batwing doors and took a long stride forward. His hands rose fast and fingers possessing the crushing power of a closing bear trap caught Keck by the shoulder. Pain numbed the man, causing his arms to drop limply to his sides. Then he felt his feet leave the floor and he was hoisted bodily into the air. With a surging heave, the blond pivoted and hurled Keck across the room. Landing on his feet, Keck still had no control over his body. He twirled around, struck and went over a table, then collided with some force against the wall.

Due to Ole Devil's unflattering comments, Dusty did not entirely trust Chisum. Nor did the rancher's employees strike the small Texan as the kind one should take at their face value. Noticing the too casual manner in which Chisum and his segundo edged away from them after Keck left, Dusty had remained alert. Although Chisum's question partly distracted the small Texan, the yelled warning from the blond giant did not come entirely as a surprise.

Knowing who had shouted, Dusty still could not prevent himself from taking a quick look at the door to assess the full extent of the danger.

Watching and waiting for Keck to make his move, Venner acted as soon as it began. Grabbing at his Colt, Venner started to slide it from leather. Just a touch slower to react, Alden also started his draw.

Certain that the blond giant could deal with Keck, Dusty saw Venner's Colt already starting to rise over the lip of the holster. There would be no time for the small Texan to draw and shoot, so he did not try. Instead he stepped closer to Venner and swept his left arm around as swiftly as he could move it. With the Colt lifting to point in his direction, Dusty's left hand struck Venner's wrist and thrust the barrel so that it no longer pointed at him. Coming across an equal speed, Dusty's right hand grasped the top of the Colt's frame and continued to turn it inwards. Pain and the threat of having his trigger-finger snapped caused Venner to relax his grip and Dusty plucked the revolver from his hand. Sliding his left hand from the trapped wrist, Dusty laid his fingers across Venner's palm and the thumb over the back of fist toward the base of the knuckles. With a deft twist, he turned Venner's elbow toward the ground and bent the captured hand towards its owner's chest. Venner let out a croak of pain, bending his torso backwards in an attempt to avoid the hurt caused by Dusty's hold.

Nor did the small Texan forget that Alden also posed a threat. Still retaining his grip on Venner's hand, Dusty lashed his right arm out and up. Just as Alden's gun cleared leather, the butt of the Colt taken from Venner smashed under his jaw. The force of its arrival snapped Alden's head back. His eyes turned glassy, and he collapsed limply to the floor.

Seeing what had happened, Targue reached for his gun. Without waiting to discover what side the segundo aimed to take in the affair, the Kid prevented him from doing it. Out flashed the bowie knife. Almost of its own volition, the clip-point of the eleven-and-a-half inch blade lined on Targue's belly ready to drive home should the need arise.

"Ain't no call for you to cut in," drawled the Kid. "Now is there?"

Targue allowed his gun to slip back into its holster. He felt, however, that his actions called for some kind of explanation.

"I thought Cap'n Fog might need some help," Targue said.

"He don't," the Kid pointed out unnecessarily and

returned his knife to its sheath.

After striking Alden down, Dusty shoved at and released Venner's hand.

"Do you want any more?" Dusty asked.

Throwing a look at Chisum for guidance, Venner thought that he saw the bald head give a quick negative shake. Which meant that any further action he took would be without the rancher's support. So he gave a shrug and replied, "Naw!"

"What's coming off, Dustine?" Goodnight demanded.

"Best ask Mark here what started it," Dusty replied, indicating the blond giant who came toward them. "I don't reckon you've met Mark Counter, Uncle Charlie. He's riding for the OD Connected."

"You'd be kin to Big Rance, I'd say," Goodnight commented, shaking hands with the blond and eyeing him from head to toe.

"Sure am, Colonel," Mark Counter agreed. "I saw that yahoo over there fixing to throw lead your way and stopped him."

"The wall stopped him," corrected the Kid. "Way you threw him, I thought he'd keep going until he had to swim the Pecos."

"Shucks," Mark grinned. "I only gave him an itty-bitty push."

"I'd hate to see you give somebody a hard shove, that being the case," Goodnight remarked, wondering how Mark came to be working for the OD Connected instead of on his father's Rover C spread.

Mark had accepted Dusty's offer of employment at the conclusion of the small Texan's mission into Mexico. Mark and the Kid had helped Dusty to carry out the task given to him by the U.S. Government. On their return to Texas, the blond giant had decided that sticking with his two friends offered better possibilities of fun and excitement than returning to help his father and three older brothers to run the family's ranch.

During the War between the States, Mark had gained a reputation for courage and as being something of a Beau Brummel. His unorthodox taste in uniforms had been much copied by the young bloods of the Confederate States Army, to the annoyance of crusty senior officers. Back at his old trade of cowhand, he tried to dress well under all conditions. A top hand with cattle, Mark was becoming spoken of for his exceptional strength and skill at roughhouse brawling. Just how good he might be with his matched Colts received much less attention, but Dusty and the Kid knew him to be very fast and accurate.

"Well, Mr. Chisum," Dusty said, turning to the rancher. "Way that Keck *hombre* acted, it looks like he knew all along that he was wide-looping the lady's cattle."

"Damn it, yes!" Chisum agreed.

"You'd not know anything about that, though?" asked the Kid innocently.

"You're damned right I didn't!" Chisum answered. "I haven't had the time to go through that herd Pitzer brought in, have I, Charlie?" Before an answer could be given, he went on, "Damn it! If they have took her cattle, they deserve all they're going to get. Take 'em to the sheriff and have 'em jailed until it's settled, Targue."

"Sure, Uncle John," the segundo answered.

"We'll amble along an' help him, huh Mark?" suggested the Kid. "Them three *pelados* might be too much for him to handle on his lonesome."

"They might at that," Mark agreed.

"Take your horses along," Dusty told his companions. "Then we'll go out and help Uncle Charlie cut the herd when you've done it."

SEVEN

Mr. Chisum's Uncle Charlie's Friend

Although Targue frowned, he raised no objections to the two Texans accompanying him. Scowling around, he called for help to tote the two unconscious hardcases down to the jail. Venner caught Chisum's eye and kept quiet.

Knowing that he could leave the safe delivery of the trio in Mark's and the Kid's hands, Goodnight suggested that the rest of the party should escort Dawn out of the saloon. Chisum said that he would collect his brother Pitzer and some of the men from Sadie's brothel, then meet the others at the herd. Watching him go, Dawn let out an indignant snort.

"Do you reckon he knew that they'd put our cattle in the herd all along?" she asked.

"I wouldn't want to go so far as say that," Dusty replied. "Time we got around the canyon and caught up to them, your stock was mixed in with the herd."

Goodnight decided to change the subject. "I'd heard that the Kid threw in with you, Dustine. It's a good thing."

"It is, for everybody," Dusty agreed. "After his pappy was killed, he didn't cotton to the smuggling game and I reckoned that the OD Connected could use him."

"He got out of that game in time," Goodnight said. "It was all right while they were running supplies in the War, but after Appomattox what they were doing became smuggling again. Sooner or later he'd've killed a revenue officer and been on the run."

Dusty nodded. Smuggling in time of peace and on the Rio Grande was a tough, dangerous business which could easily have seen the Kid driven into a life of real, serious crime.

"Anyways, Lon'll be real useful on this drive you're planning, Uncle Charlie. So'll Mark, he's real good with cattle. And we'll see how it's done."

Listening to the men, Dawn wondered what was so special about the next trail drive Goodnight planned to make. Since the War ended, he had been taking cattle to various Army posts. More than that, most cowhands already possessed experience in moving stock from place to place. So she wondered why the OD Connected needed to send its segundo and two men to learn how to handle a herd on the trail. Yet she could not think how to satisfy her curiosity without causing offense.

Looking at the small Texan as they left the saloon, Dawn tried to reconcile his appearance with his reputation. She had always thought of Dusty as the tall, handsome, dashing cavalry leader who ran the hated Yankees ragged across the Arkansas battlefront. It came as something of a shock to meet him. Then she recalled how he had seemed to loom over the others when facing Keck and the two hardcases, and the speed with which he had moved when dealing with them. A man like Dusty Fog could not be judged in mere feet and inches. Came trouble, he stood tallest of them all.

Going to collect her *bayo-tigre*, she noticed that the white and bloodbay stallions had been taken from their places. When Dusty walked up to and freed the big paint, she guessed that the other two horses which had so interested her must belong to his friends. Thinking back to the stories she had heard of the Ysabel Kid, she remembered that he was said always to ride a white stallion credited with being a very effective second set of eyes, ears and nostrils for him.

"That's a real fine, hoss, Cap'n Fog," Dawn remarked, noticing that he carried a short rifle of some sort in his saddleboot. "I'll bet he's a fighter."

"He's all of that," Dusty agreed. Before he had ridden and mastered the big paint, it had thrown and crippled Ole Devil Hardin.* "Why'd you gather those cattle, Miss—?"

"Sutherland," the girl supplied, blushing a little. "Dawn Sutherland. It's about time for the buyer from the Brazoria hide-and-tallow factory to come around. So we'd got a bunch of steers gathered and held to sell to him."

Dusty could imagine that the Sutherlands had a serious need of the money the cattle would bring. Supporting the Confederacy in the War, the people of the Lone Star State found themselves holding a

---

*Told in *The Fastest Gun in Texas*.

worthless currency with the South's defeat. In that respect Dusty's kin had been fortunate. Due to the foresight of Ole Devil, most of the clan's wealth had been in gold or invested over seas. So the OD Connected possessed sufficient funds to tide it over. Others had not been so lucky. The loss of the small herd would have dire results unless the steers could be recovered.

"We'll see that you get them all back," Dusty promised.

Going out to the herd, Dusty explained to Goodnight why his arrival had been delayed. He, Mark and the Kid had been helping a family of mustangers catch wild horses and fight against a murderous band of Mexican *bandidos.*† On reaching the herd, Goodnight decided that they would delay the cutting until Chisum arrived. Before he came, Dusty's two companions rode up and Dawn saw that she had guessed correctly about their horses. Impatient to find her cattle, the girl rode off to circle the herd. Watching her go, the Kid addressed the small Texan.

"They're locked away, Dusty, and I'd say that they'll stay that way if the sheriff has anything to do with it."

"Ward Kater's a good peace officer, Kid," Goodnight put in. "He'll do whatever's right."

"Thing I don't like's how easy those three yahoos took it," Mark commented. "You'd've expected them to act a mite worried at least; but if they were, they sure didn't show it."

"Maybe they're figuring on somebody helping them," Dusty suggested. "Did Targue say anything to them?"

"Only to shut their mouths, not to tell lies and to get

†Told in *.44 Caliber Man.*

into the cells," Mark replied. "They went in quiet enough after that."

"Where's Targue now?" Goodnight inquired.

"Allowed he was going back for his boss," Mark answered. "The sheriff says he'll hold those three yahoos until we've cut the herd. Then, if the gal wants it that way, she can go in and swear a complaint against them."

"I reckon she'll want to," Dusty guessed. "She's pot-boiling mad and I can't say I blame her. I'm getting real interested to see what we find when we cut that herd."

"And me," Goodnight admitted. "Until you boys cut in, I'll admit I was just a mite suspicious about her coming here with that story."

"How come, Uncle Charlie?"

"I'm not the only one with my eye on the Army beef contracts, Dustine. There were a couple of Yankee businessmen at Sumner and they looked some down in the mouth when I got the first contract. So I wondered if maybe they could have fixed up this play to make trouble for me."

"They didn't know we were around," Dusty said. "It's not likely they'd've gone to the trouble of having the girl hide while they drove off the herd."

"I know," agreed Goodnight. "So it looks like she's telling the truth."

At that moment the girl returned and brought her *bayo-tigre* to a halt.

"I reckon I've seen some of mine," she announced. "There's a big *golondrino* muley I'd know any old place on the other side of the herd."

Although *golondrino*—dunnish brown merging into black, with white speckles or blotches on the rump—was not an unusual color, a muley's hornless head made it noticeable.

"You want for me to go and cut it out, Dusty?" Mark asked.

"Best leave it until Chisum gets here," the small Texan decided.

"Which'll be right soon," drawled the Kid. "He's coming right now, and bringing company."

"Seven of 'em, not counting John and Pitzer," Goodnight went on, studying the approaching party. "Got their chuck wagon along, and the remuda's following."

"They're an ornery-looking bunch," Dawn remarked.

"Real ornery," Dusty agreed. "How about the four fellers with the herd, Uncle Charlie?"

"They're my boys," the rancher answered.

"Damned if we don't near on have 'em outnumbered," said the Kid and looked at the butt of the rifle in his saddleboot.

"Injuns never learn to count, ma'am," Mark explained to Dawn.

"Looks that way," the girl smiled.

"Leave it, you danged *Pehnane* slit-eye!" Dusty hissed as the Kid bent in a casual manner toward the rifle. "Mr. Chisum's Uncle Charlie's friend."

"You got friends like him, you don't need enemies," grinned the Kid and straightened up empty-handed.

"I'll tell you whether he's my friend after we've cut the herd," Goodnight growled, his face tight-lipped and grim, and waved his hand.

At their boss's signal, the four cowhands left their places around the herd and converged on him. They were tanned, leathery men with low-hanging guns; but not the surly, hardcase kind hired by Chisum. Asking no questions, the four Swinging G cowhands took positions ideally suited to backing Goodnight in any play he made.

Drawing nearer, Chisum's hands studied the Swinging G and OD Connected men.

"We're going to cut the herd," Goodnight announced and saw the disconcerted way in which Pitzer—a dandy-dressed, younger edition of his brother—and the Chisum cowhands exchanged glances. "I want all the D4S cattle you find brought out here."

"You heard Colonel Charlie," Chisum called. "Let's get to it."

"I'd say it'd be quicker if we work in pairs, Uncle Charlie," Dusty put in. "You go with Mr. Chisum, I'll side Targue and Mark'll help Pitzer."

"That's how we'll do it," Goodnight agreed, grinning inwardly as he caught the purpose of Dusty's idea. "Two men can see a whole heap more than one."

Giving Chisum no time to organize a protest, Goodnight assigned the Kid, Dawn or one of his men to work with each of the Long Rail hands. The girl found herself paired up with a lantern-jawed hardcase who eyed her in a cold, threatening manner. For a moment she felt just a touch of fear. Once among the cattle it would be easy to arrange for an "accident" to happen. A quick, unseen push to topple her from the *bayo-tigre*'s back and her chances of escape would be slight.

Then Dawn saw the Kid rein in his white stallion at her companion's side.

"Look after the lady, feller," the dark youngster purred in that gentle tone so well known and feared in the lower Rio Grande border country. "Just a lil favor for me. I'll be close by to thank you."

Which meant, as Dawn and—from the expression on his face—the hardcase knew, "Don't try anything. If the girl gets hurt in any way, so will you, only a whole heap worse."

"We'll start round the other side," Dawn decided and, with the Kid hovering menacingly in the background, the Long Rail hardcase raised no objections.

Circling around the herd, the girl watched until she saw the *golondrino* muley. Experience had taught her that longhorns tended to be clannish. Even when mixed in a large herd, they would try to stick close to familiar faces among the strangers. That ought to make cutting out her stock a comparatively simple task.

Pointing out the muley to the man, Dawn edged her *bayo-tigre* into the herd. With the Kid's threat still echoing in his ears, the hardcase followed. While not a praying man under normal conditions, he came mighty close to requesting that divine providence keep the girl from harm. If she met with even a genuine accident, the Long Rail hand figured himself to have mighty short life expectancy.

While Dawn eased the *golondrino* clear of the herd, the hardcase spotted other cattle bearing her father's D4S brand. On their way from town, Chisum had given certain instructions. Yet the hardcase saw no way in which he might carry them out, not with the girl watching his every move. So he accepted the inevitable and forced another of the Sutherland longhorns into the open.

Not far from where Dawn was working the Kid and his partner helped to cut out more of the D4S cattle. It came as something of a surprise for the girl to see that Dusty, Mark and Goodnight made no attempt to join her where her cattle were concentrated. Instead they seemed more concerned with combing the less productive areas of the herd. Once she noticed Chisum pointing her way and clearly making a suggestion that he and Goodnight should join her, but he was refused.

The bearded rancher's face grew into colder, grimmer lines as the work continued.

Instead of being allowed to skim through the herd and produce a few of the D4S cattle, each of the Long Rail men found himself accompanied by a rider who meant to see the work was done correctly. So the combing-out process was very thorough. At the end of it something over a hundred steer, all with a large D4S brand burned indelibly on their left flanks, stood clear of the main bunch.

With the work completed, the two parties gathered behind their respective leaders. In view of what she had seen while working among the cattle, Dawn felt sure that a showdown between Goodnight and Chisum was close at hand.

"I'd say that's all you lost, Miss Sutherland," Chisum stated, shoving back his hat and mopping his bald head with a cheap bandana. "And I'd like to say that I don't know how they got mixed in with my herd."

"Maybe Pitzer can tell us," Goodnight suggested coldly.

"Sure I can," the younger Chisum brother agreed. "Them three fellers drove 'em in just's we was bedding down for the night. Targue and me was on the other side of the herd and Keck just shoved 'em straight in with our'n. Allowed they was a bunch of mavericks when I asked."

To anybody who knew Pitzer's character, the answer was feasible. He had a disclination to work and would be unlikely to investigate the trio's story too closely if doing so required effort on his part. Unfortunately the combing of the herd had been very thorough and brought out a major discrepancy in young Chisum's glib tale.

"Did the same thing happen with all those Bench P steers I saw?" Mark asked. "And to those Rocking N and Double Two stock you've got along?"

"Or to the Flying H an' Lazy F stuff that's there?" the Kid went on.

"I saw *some* mavericks," Dusty continued. "Even a few maps of Mexico.* Fact being, Mr. Chisum, the only brand I didn't see any place in that herd was the Long Rail."

Silence, broken only by the slight restless moving of the horses, dropped ominously after Dusty's blunt statement and the two sides eyed each other warily. Every man present, and the girl, knew the implications behind the small Texan's words. So the hired hands waited and watched to see how their respective employers wanted the situation to develop.

Slouching in his saddle, Chisum slowly thrust away his bandana. He knew that he must pick his words very carefully if he hoped to steer clear of being held responsible for his brother's actions. Avoiding trouble unless he held the whip hand had always been Chisum's way. Making a quick assessment of the situation, he knew that he did not hold it at that moment. Backed by the three OD Connected riders and his own cowhands, Goodnight had a fighting force to be reckoned with. The four Swinging G cowhands could be counted on to stand by their boss from soda to hock no matter how tough the going. Chisum had no such faith in his hired hardcases, especially those who came with Targue. So the bald rancher decided to try to ease out of the difficulty peaceably.

"You said that you needed the eleven hundred head in a real hurry, Charlie," Chisum pointed out in his most unctuous and placating manner. "So Brother Pitzer allowed it'd be quicker to round up some strays

---

*Map of Mexico: large complicated brand used by Mexican ranchers.

instead of going right back to the Long Rail and gathering our stuff."

A neat way out, in Chisum's opinion, laying all the blame on his younger brother's incompetent shoulders. Pitzer scowled at the words, but he had grown accustomed to being used as a whipping-boy and kept quiet.

"Most of those strays have brands on them, Mr. Chisum," Dusty reminded.

On the open range, a bull, cow, calf or steer belonged to whoever's brand it carried, no matter where it might be found. Left to forage for themselves all year round, Texas longhorns were great travelers. So the code of ownership by brand rather than location gave protection to the ranchers.

"Likely the boys were a mite over-eager," Chisum answered blandly. "Them wanting to help Colonel Charlie out of a tight spot and all."

"Helping out's not what I'd call it," Dusty stated.

"Or me!" Goodnight growled, giving complete backing to his nephew's words. "What was the idea, Chisum, mix them in with my shipping herd and hope that I didn't notice the brands?"

"Do you reckon I'd do a meanness like that, Charlie?" Chisum asked in tones of pained disappointment. "After all the time we've knowed each other."

"You didn't have them brought here because they need the exercise," Goodnight answered.

"Charlie, Charlie!" Chisum sighed. "We've been doing business together for a fair time now—"

"And in all that time I've never taken anything but straight-branded cattle from you," Goodnight reminded him. "I'm not starting to buy stolen cattle now."

"Can't say's how I like what you just said, Charlie.

But I'm not fixing to fight a real good friend over a lil misunderstanding."

"That's not the name I'd put to what you've done today," Goodnight grunted, nodding toward the herd.

"I'm not arguing with you, Charlie," Chisum insisted. "If you don't want these-here cattle—"

"I don't!"

"Then that's all there is to it. Nobody can say that John Chisum tried to force his will on other folks. I'll just take the rest of them back where they come from and turn 'em loose again. Only I don't figure on bringing you any more."

EIGHT

It's Not As Easy As All That

Being aware of the importance of his cattle to Goodnight's plans, Chisum might have hoped his ultimatum would force a change of heart. If so, he was doomed to be disappointed. Goodnight was a scrupulously honest man and unwilling to sacrifice his principles at any cost.

Although Chisum had, up to that point, been completely honest in his dealing with Goodnight, the same did not apply to his treatment of other people. In the past Goodnight had tolerated Chisum despite the other's faults, knowing something of the reason why he had turned into a unscrupulous miser. All that altered when Chisum attempted such a blatant piece of dishonesty as delivering a herd which consisted almost entirely of stolen animals.

"That suits me fine," Goodnight answered calmly. "I only want to buy honest stock."

"Do you reckon that you can do without me and my cattle, Charlie?" Chisum asked, switching his tactics.

Alert for trouble, Dusty watched the other men rather than the two ranchers. He noticed Targue squirming uneasily as the conversation continued and wondered why.

"I'll damned well make a stab at it!" Goodnight stated, although he knew the disastrous effect the words might have on his scheme.

"All these boys I brought along to help with your drive'll pull out if I go," Chisum went on and Dusty saw Targue's uneasiness increasing.

"That's something I'm going to have to chance," Goodnight replied. "Just get those cattle off my range as fast as you can."

"Have it your way, Charlie," Chisum sighed, although Targue showed some relief. "Get them moved out, Pitzer."

"How about your three men in Graham jail, Mr. Chisum?" Dusty asked.

"They stole the cattle deliberate from the young lady, Cap'n Fog," the bald rancher answered. "I'm going to let the legal law hand them their needings."

With that, Chisum turned his horse and rode after his departing men. Dropping back, Targue ranged his mount alongside the rancher's. Quickly the segundo glanced over his shoulder to make sure that his words would not carry to the ears of Goodnight's party. Apart from sending two men to handle Dawn's cattle while the herd moved off, the bearded rancher showed no signs of movement and displayed no interest in Chisum's crew.

"I thought you'd spoil it all," Targue commented.

"Going on like you did to Goodnight."

"Did, huh?" Chisum replied mildly.

"Sure. Way you kept reminding him what he stood to lose. I figured he'd take the herd after all."

"You don't know Charlie Goodnight like I do. More I'd've argued, the more set he'd've got at doing the right thing way he sees it. So I kept stirring him up and done what whoever's paying you wanted doing."

"How's that?" Targue grunted.

"Charlie's shy this eleven hundred head on what he's contracted to deliver. Unless he's on the trail in ten days at most, he'll not reach Fort Sumner by the end of June. That means he's got to raise a thousand head or more before he starts. And he can't move'em without my men helping him. Which all amounts to one thing."

"What?" asked Targue.

"That I've done what's wanted."

"Yeah," admitted the segundo. "I reckon you have. So I'll give you the money as soon as we're clear of Graham."

A faint grin twisted Chisum's lips and his face took on its expression of benevolent innocence that only came when he was about to spring the trap on a shady deal.

"It's not as easy as all that," the rancher warned.

"How do you mean?" Targue growled.

"I stood to make a fair heap of money with Charlie. More than your bosses've paid me— "

"Only you'd spoiled that chance when Pitzer lost the herd."

"We could've likely come through," Chisum insisted. "Only you made me an easier offer. I took it and done my share. But I've been thinking a mite about it."

"Such as?" Targue muttered suspiciously.

By that time the herd, chuck wagon and remuda were on the move. Chisum waved a languid hand toward the trail crew.

"There's money behind you, Wally. More'n I can make working with Charlie, he's got too many notions of what's wrong and right for other folks to suit me. Now I don't reckon that'd apply to your bosses. Likely we'll get along."

"You know 'em then?"

"Not yet. But I'm going to. I'll trail along with you and meet 'em. If they're getting contracts from the Army, they'll likely need a good man to help them fill 'em."

"I dunno about that—" Targue began.

"Put it this way, Wally," interrupted Chisum. "Happen you don't take me to meet 'em, I'll just naturally have to take *you* back to Charlie Goodnight and tell him's how I learned you'd hoodwinked Pitzer into wide-looping these cattle."

For all their being spoken in a gentle, almost apologetic voice, the words were charged with menace. Cold anger creased Targue's face and his hand crept toward his holstered revolver.

"You reckon I'd keep quiet about your side of it?" Targue asked.

"Sure you will," Chisum answered calmly. "I'd hate like hell to do it, Wally, but if I took you back you'd be dead. Nigger Frank there's got his scatter lined on you right now."

Twisting his head, Targue saw Chisum's Negro cook allowing the team of the chuck wagon to amble along while nursing an evil-looking double-barreled shotgun which pointed in the segundo's direction.

"My men—!" Targue began.

"Real nice boys, all of 'em," Chisum replied. "Why, they'd have no sympathy for anybody's made trouble for good ole Uncle John."

Having seen the way in which Chisum could influence even surly hardcases and win them over, Targue did not doubt the comment. Loyal only as long as the money lasted, their kind would change sides quickly enough. Slowly a grudging admiration filled Targue and he let out a chuckle.

"Know something, Uncle John?" he said. "I reckon the bosses could use a gent like you—And even if they couldn't, I figure we're smart enough between us to come out of this winning."

"So do I, Wally," Chisum purred. "So do I. Say though, Fog had a point about them three fellers of your'n we've left in the poky."

"How'd you mean?"

"They might start talking when they hear that we've gone."

"They won't," Targue assured the rancher. "I saw to their needings afore I came looking for you and Pitzer."

"You're a smart young cuss, Wally," complimented Chisum. "Seems a real pity to waste these cattle, though. 'Specially with the Army paying good money for 'em. Reckon your bosses can use 'em—happen we do something about the brands, that is."

"I reckon they can," Targue answered. "Only we'd best swing off to the north as soon as we're out of Goodnight's sight. Somebody besides that gal might be looking for cattle they've lost."

Watching Chisum follow his men, Dawn let out a low sigh of relief. Then she remembered that there had been other brands represented among the herd.

"Shouldn't we have taken all the cattle instead of

letting him go off with them?" she asked.

"I don't reckon he'd've let them go," the Kid drawled, having drawn his rifle and sitting holding it downward on the side of his stallion away from the departing trail herd.

"That's for sure," Dusty agreed. "If we'd tried, likely Chisum would've dug his heels in. That'd mean shooting—"

"Which, in turn'd mean the whole bunch, including yours, would stampede," Mark continued. "And that wouldn't've done any of us any good."

"Maybe Chisum'll do like he said and turn them loose," Dusty went on. "I don't reckon he'll have anywhere that he can sell them."

"Damn it!" Goodnight barked. "I never figured that Chisum'd pull a game like this on me."

"How'd it happen, Uncle Charlie?" Dusty wanted to know.

"Pitzer was bringing eleven hundred head here to complete my herd. Only him and his crew left the cattle while they went into some town on the way. While they were gone, the herd stampeded and they lost it. So John went off to send Pitzer to gather more. I must admit I thought they'd worked fast when they got back so soon, but I'd never start to think he'd pull a play like this."

"Maybe he figured that you'd do the same as he would, take the herd and be pleased to get it," Mark suggested.

"I'd've thought he knew me too well for that," Goodnight answered.

"It could have come out badly for you, happen he'd mixed that bunch in with your shipping herd, Uncle Charlie," Dusty said quietly. "Their owners and other folks would blame you for the theft."

"Yeah," agreed the Kid. "And some folks get real touchy about getting stole from. I wonder what Chisum and that hard-faced cuss're talking about?"

"Could be where'd be the best place to turn loose those cattle, but I doubt it. Do you want for Lon to trail after them a ways, Uncle Charlie?"

"Nope. John Chisum might be tricky, but he's not fool enough to come back looking for trouble with me."

"I'm real sorry if I came between you and your friend, Colonel," Dawn put in.

Turning, the rancher smiled at the girl. "It'd've come sooner or later, Miss Sutherland. How do you figure on getting your cattle back home?"

Dawn gave a shrug and replied, "Likely I can pick up a couple of fellers around town to help me."

"You could," Goodnight admitted. "Only I don't take to the notion of you picking out a couple of strangers. Trouble being that I'm going to need every man I've got for rounding up eleven hundred head to replace Chisum's herd."

"I'll be all right," Dawn stated and wished that she felt as confident as she tried to sound.

"How important is it that you get those cattle back home, Miss Sutherland?" Dusty inquired. "I mean, does it matter to a day or so?"

"That buyer'll be around by the end of the week," she replied and, after a brief pause, continued, "Miss Sutherland makes me sound real old. Couldn't you say 'Dawn' instead?"

"I reckon I could, if you call me 'Dusty.' If the buyer'll not be around until the end of the week, I reckon you could spend the night at Uncle Charlie's house and still be home in time."

"It's a bachelor spread, Miss Sutherland," Goodnight warned. "But if you'd care to stay, you'll be more than welcome. I'll ask the Dilwotts from the store to come out for the night—"

"Why?" Dawn smiled.

"So that Mrs. Dilwott can act as a chaperone for you."

"If I figured I was going to need one, I'd've said 'no' from the start."

"Danged if I know whether that's a compliment to me or not," Goodnight said with a frosty grin.

"Nor me," drawled Mark. "I'd say that all depends on how old you are."

"Which's just about what I'd expect one of Big Rance Counter's sons to say," Goodnight sniffed. "Shall we get going, we can bed your cattle down by the house, Miss Sutherland."

"It'd be as well," Dusty agreed and turned in his saddle to look after the Goodnight herd. "They're pushing the cattle a mite, aren't they?"

"Maybe they don't like the company around here," suggested the Kid.

"You're sure you don't want him to trail after them, Uncle Charlie?" Dusty asked in a disgusted tone.

"I don't," the rancher replied, then a thought struck him. "What do you intend to do about those three fellers, Miss Dawn?"

"I'm not fixing to do anything," the girl answered. "I've got my stock—"

"Why not go ,in and swear the complaint against them?" Dusty interrupted.

"I don't want to make a fuss," she replied. "Do you reckon I ought to?"

"I reckon you should," Dusty confirmed. "Even if you don't push it through all the way, it'll be interesting to hear what those three jaspers have to say. Especially when they hear that their boss's pulled out and left them."

"You figure they might do some talking, Dusty?" Mark inquired.

"I'm hoping that they do," Dusty admitted. "Take my gear out to the ranch for me, Mark."

"And mine," drawled the Kid.

"You lend a hand with the herd," Dusty ordered with a grin. "I don't want Dawn getting wrong ideas about Rio Hondo County by associating with varmints like you."

"She couldn't get *wrong* ideas about Rio Hondo County," sniffed the Kid and slid his rifle into the saddleboot.

For the first time Dawn noticed that the Kid held a repeater. It looked like a Henry, yet had a wooden foregrip along the lower part of the magazine tube. While riding into town with Dusty, she learned that all the three OD Connected men carried similar weapons. Known at that time as the New Improved Henry, the type of rifle grew to fame as the Winchester Model of 1866 or, due to its brass frame, "the old yellowboy." Dusty, Mark and the Kid had been given the guns during the mission into Mexico. While his friends selected rifles, Dusty had chosen the shorter carbine model.

Approaching the jail, they could see no sign of life. Although the sun was starting to set, the lamps in the sheriff's office had not yet been lit.

"Likely the sheriff's gone ho—" Dusty began.

The words chopped off as the office's front door flew open and Keck came out. With his Metropolitan revolver in his hand, he stopped and gazed at the approaching riders. Recognition flared on his face, twisting it into hate-filled lines. Behind him, Venner and Alden also emerged from the building. Like Keck, they were armed. Venner had an Army Colt, while Alden clutched a double-barreled shotgun.

At the first sight of the three men, Dusty knew knew they must be escaping. Released prisoners would not come through the door holding weapons and in such an alert, wolf-cautious manner.

So, even as Keck started to raise the revolver, Dusty acted. Wanting the girl clear of the danger area, Dusty jerked his left boot from its stirrup. With a whooping yell, he kicked the *bayo-tigre* in the ribs and continued to swing his leg forward, then over his saddlehorn. A spirited animal, Dawn's horse showed its objection to the treatment by leaping forward, and galloping by the front of the jail. Slapping the paint's flanks as he dropped clear, Dusty sent it running after the *bayo-tigre*. On landing, he flashed his hands across to the butts of the Colts.

Flame licked from Keck's Metropolitan. Dusty's hat flew from his head with a hole in its crown, to be caught and held by its storm-strap. Already holding his matched Army Colts, he went instantly into what would come to be known as the gunfighter's crouch. Legs slightly bent on spread-apart feet, body inclined forward, Dusty made no attempt to lift either revolver above waist level. Even as the storm-strap tugged against his neck, he cut loose with a shot from the right-hand revolver and aimed it by instinctive alignment. A conical .44 bullet spiked into Keck's throat before he could draw back the Metropolitan's hammer for another shot. Reeling back, he almost crashed into the two men following him.

Alden flung himself to the left, letting Keck sprawl between him and Venner as he tried to line the shotgun on Dusty. Going aside in a fast dive, Dusty just managed to pass beyond the spreading pattern of buckshot which belched from the right-hand barrel of the shot-gun. The small Texan landed rolling, seeing Venner's Colt starting to swing in his direction. Having missed with his attempt from waist high, Alden began to swing the shotgun shoulderwards. There would be no time for Dusty to stop both his attackers.

Brain working as fast as it could, Dusty analyzed the situation and thought up a possible solution. Of the two, Alden held the more dangerous weapon. Maybe Venner would miss with the Colt, but there was far less chance of Alden doing so a second time with the shotgun.

With that in mind, Dusty fired his left-hand Colt as he landed on his side. He missed and continued to roll, twisting himself over with desperate speed but not in panic. Looking along the barrel of his left-hand Colt, he found it was lined at Alden's chest. Satisfied, Dusty squeezed the trigger. On the heels of the revolver's shot, the other weapon boomed. Only by a fraction of a second had Dusty beaten Alden to the shot, but it proved to be sufficient. Deflected slightly when the .44 ball struck home, the second barrel of the shotgun sent its charge on their way. Ploughing into the hard-packed surface of the street with a solid "whomp!" the buckshot balls threw geysers of dirt up to patter against Dusty's shirt. Continuing his roll, Dusty saw Alden stumble back and let the shotgun drop. Blood was trickling down the hardcase's shirt from a hole in its left breast and the truculent expression had at last been wiped from his face.

Startled though she had been by Dusty's actions, Dawn's long experience at riding kept her in the saddle. Nor did she allow the horse to continue running unchecked. Regaining control of it, she started to rein it around. At the same time she twisted her right hand back to grip and draw the Cooper revolver from its holster. Trained to use firearms by her parents, she acted swiftly. Seeing that Dusty needed help, she raised, sighted and fired the revolver.

Advancing to the edge of the sidewalk for a clearer shot at Dusty, Venner became suddenly aware of the girl's intervention. Splinters erupted from the top of the hitching rail close to his empty hand as a bullet ploughed into the wood. The small Texan's Colt was roaring out its challenge to the shotgun, and the sickening sound of lead driving into flesh rose from close by. Too close for it to be Dusty Fog who had caught the bullet, which left only Alden to be the victim.

Venner paused briefly, wondering if he should run in the girl's direction. If he shot her, he could grab her horse and made good his escape. Only, doing so would be extremely dangerous. Judging by the manner in which she thumb-cocked the Cooper on its recoil, that girl knew how to handle a gun. She did not act scared, but showed every sign of knowing the score.

Reaching a decision with commendable speed, Venner turned to his left and darted in front of his dying companion. Down the street, a horse was hitched before a barber's shop. So he raced along the sidewalk toward the animal. As he approached his goal, he saw the sheriff run out of a store across the street.

Unlike many of the men appointed as peace officers by the corrupt, inefficient Davis Administration which the Union Government had put in control of Texas, Sheriff Ward Kater enforced the law. Having heard the shooting, he appeared ready for trouble with his Colt drawn and cocked in hand.

"Hold it!" Kater yelled, bounding from the sidewalk.

"Go to hell!" Venner screeched and sent a bullet across the street.

Which showed mighty poor sense when dealing with a man trained in Captain Jack Cureton's now-disbanded company of Texas Rangers. With the smooth speed gained fighting an assortment of bad men during the War between the States, Kater threw up his gun and returned Venner's fire. The escaping man cried out in pain as lead caught him. Stumbling backwards, he still retained his hold on the Colt and tried to use it again. Once more Kater's revolver cracked. Struck in the skull by the second bullet, Venner crumpled lifeless to the sun-warped sidewalk boards.

"Catch my saddle, Dawn!" Dusty yelled, coming to his feet and wanting to keep the girl out of harm's way."

Deciding that there was no further danger to Dusty, she turned to obey. The request made by the small Texan was one often given by an unhorsed cowhand. While the horse which threw him usually belonged to the rancher who hired him, the saddle was always the cowhand's own property and its loss not to be contemplated. So the girl rode after and caught Dusty's paint.

After removing Dawn from the line of further fire, Dusty sprang on to the sidewalk and across it to enter the sheriff's office. His right-hand Colt aimed at Keck's sprawling shape; but one glance told him there would be no further danger from the man.

Looking across the room, Dusty saw a figure lying face down in one of the cells. Then the sheriff appeared at the door, also holding a cocked weapon.

Halting, Kater studied the scene for a moment, then

gave Dusty a long, searching glance. "You're Captain Fog, aren't you?"

"Sure."

"Colonel Charlie told me you were coming. Looks like you arrived just at the right time."

"I had to kill these two," Dusty remarked as the sheriff opened the cell and entered to kneel by the groaning man. "Did you get the other alive?"

"No," Kater admitted. "It's a pity they're all dead. I'd like to know where they got the guns."

NINE

Eight Cents a Pound, On The Hoof

The clock in the corner of Goodnight's comfortably furnished living room chimed eleven as he and his guests gathered before the fireplace at the conclusion of their belated meal. Dusty and Dawn had not reached the ranch until shortly before ten, due to the small Texan assisting the sheriff in trying to discover how the prisoners obtained the weapons used while making their escape bid. Dusty told his uncle, the Kid, Mark and the girl about the investigation.

"Seems that Keck and his pards waited for Sheriff Kater to leave the office and hoped he'd be down to his home before they made their move," Dusty explained. "Then Keck called the deputy over and asked him for a match. Only as he was taking it out, Keck threw down on him. It was a choice of opening the door or getting shot, so the deputy opened up. Keck whomped him over the head as soon as he'd done it. The other two helped themselves to the deputy's Colt and one of the office scatterguns, their own being locked in the safe, and headed for the tall timber."

"And walked out of the front door to find us riding along the street toward them," Dawn went on. She gave a slight shudder. "That Keck sure looked mean when he saw us."

"Where'd Keck get the gun he used to make that deputy open up?" inquired the Kid. "He for sure didn't have it on him when he went into the cell."

"That's for sure," Goodnight agreed. "Ward Kater's too smart a peace officer to make a mistake like that."

"It was Keck's hideout gun. The one he tried to use on us at the Demon Rum," Dusty replied. "Did any of you see who picked it up?"

"I was watching Chisum," Goodnight excused himself.

"It'd already gone when I looked for it," Mark went on. "But there'd been a fair slew of folks moving around and Targue was pushing to get them three yahoos tossed into the poky, so I didn't take time out to ask who'd got it. Maybe somebody at the saloon saw who took it."

"If they did, they're not admitting to it," Dusty answered. "The sheriff asked about it."

"Targue went around the back of the jailhouse after we'd seen them put into the cells," the blond giant remarked. "Allowed he was headed for Sadie's place to pick up Chisum's men and take them out to the herd."

"That'd be the shortest way for him to go from the sheriff's office to Sadie's," Goodnight said.

"Now me," Mark grinned. "I wouldn't know where a place like Sadie's'd be."

"You sure you're Big Rance's son?" Goodnight sniffed. "Anyways, I reckon we can leave it in Ward Kater's hands. I didn't have you boys come out here to run around playing at being lawmen."

Watching Dusty, Mark and the Kid, Dawn saw them sit just a little straighter in their chairs and show a mite more interest. She stirred restlessly on her seat and the movement brought the rancher's attention to her.

"If you're tired, Dawn—" Goodnight began.

"I am a mite," she admitted, wondering if he would use it as an excuse to get her out of the room.

"It's late all right," the rancher said. "But I'd like you to stay a while longer if you will. What I have to say to Dustine might interest your pappy."

"I'm not all that sleepy," the girl smiled. "It's not my first late night.'

"*Bueno*," Goodnight grunted and turned toward his nephew. "Do you know why Ole Devil sent you here, Dustine?"

"I only know what you said in your letter," Dusty replied. "That you're making a big drive to Fort Sumner real soon and figured Uncle Devil might want to send the floating outfit along to see how it's done."

After finishing his answer, Dusty looked expectantly at his uncle. So did Dawn, realizing that there must be something more than that behind the rancher's suggestion. It seemed hardly likely that Old Devil Hardin would send his segundo and members of the OD Connected's floating outfit all the way to Young County merely to witness something they had already gathered experience in doing.

Dawn's father did not run a large enough spread to

need the services of a floating outfit, but she knew what the term meant. On the big ranches like the OD Connected a group of four to six men, top hands every one, were employed to work on the distant sections of the range. Taking along food either in a chuckwagon, or "greasy sack" on the back of a mule, they spent long periods away from the main house and acted as a kind of mobile ranch crew. During the ride from Graham, Dawn had learned that Ole Devil had not only sent Dusty, Mark and the Kid, but that two more of the floating outfits were following with their remuda.

"Who do you sell your cattle to at the OD Connected, Dustine?" Goodnight inquired when sure he had his audience's attention.

"The Army take a few," the small Texan replied. "But most go to the hide-and-tallow factories at Brazoria or Quintana."

"We'll sell to anybody who'll buy, Colonel," Dawn answered when Goodnight repeated the question to her. "Which means the hide-and-tallow buyer, mostly."

"And you're getting paid—?" Goodnight went on.

"Three dollars a head. At that price, pappy has to sell all he can to keep us going."

"It's the same all across Texas," Dusty said. "We get around the same price, four dollars tops. Or eight if we trail them to the factory. We did it one time, took five hundred head along. When we'd paid off the trail hands and other expenses, we figured it wasn't worth the trouble of doing it."

"Did you ever see one of them factories, Colonel Charlie?" Mark asked.

"Can't say I ever did," the rancher admitted.

"They've got gangs of Negroes killing the cattle, bulls, steers, cows and calves, skinning them, stripping out the tallow and sending what's left, including the meat, down chutes into the Brazos," Mark told him grimly.

"There're catfish so well fed they're bigger'n Mississippi alligator-gars downstream from the factory at Brazoria," the Kid went on. "And folk daren't go swimming in the sea below Quintana because of the sharks that come in after the factory leavings."

"There's no other place to sell the stock," Dawn reminded the men bitterly. "I've heard that it's been tried and didn't come off."

"Feller called Kil Vickers thought he'd got the answer," Dusty remarked. "Took two hundred and fifty head to Rockport and shipped them by coast-boat to New Orleans. Time he'd finished paying for their feeding on the boat and all, he found he'd lost two dollars-fifty a head on the deal."

"Shangai Pierce did a mite better though," Mark pointed out. "Just after the War he drove a big bunch of his 'sea-lions'* clear across Louisiana to New Orleans and sold them for a fair price."

"Trouble being that those 'sea-lions' of his're raised in swamp country," Dusty objected. "Open-plains beef like we handle'd never make it."

"Could, happen we knowed how to train 'em to swing across the bog holes like Shangai's stock done it," argued the Kid, keeping a straight, sober face.

"Swing over the bog holes!" Dawn snorted, sensing that the comment had been directed her way. "You'll never get *me* to believe *that*!"

"I'm only telling you what Mark allows Shangai told him," protested the Kid. "That's what he told you, wasn't it, Mark?"

---

*Sea-Lions: cattle reared in the coastal districts of Texas.

"Why he crossed his heart and hoped to vote Republican if it wasn't true," Mark agreed. "Then he told me how his old 'sea-lions' went through the cypress swamps by jumping from root to root. And when they came to a real deep bog hole, they'd swing across it by hooking their horns in a wistaria or mustang grape-vine. He allowed that *that* was some sight to see."

"Yah? Any feller who'd spin windies like them deserves to vote Republican," Dawn scoffed, then looked pointedly at Mark and the Kid. "And anybody fool *loco* enough to believe him most likely does."

Chuckles broke from the men and Dawn rose in their esteem by virtue of her reply. Dusty wondered why his uncle had asked her to stay and listen to his business.

"Shipping by sea, or trailing to New Orleans and selling's no answer for us," Goodnight pointed out when the youngsters stopped funning. "The costs of doing either would eat up every red cent of the profits."

"What's the answer then, Uncle Charlie?" asked Dusty. "Go on selling to the hide-and-tallow factories until the ranges are stripped bare of cattle. And that's what'll come if the prices stay so low that folks have to sell off breeding stock the way they're being forced to do."

"I know," Goodnight answered. "The Army only want steers, which's why I'm in favor of dealing with them."

"Trouble being the Army in Texas doesn't need much beef," Dusty pointed out. "And New Mexico's a mite out of the way for us ranchers down in the southeast. 'Sides which, if everybody trails herds to Fort Sumner, they'll flood the market and the price'll drop to nothing."

Goodnight nodded soberly. As he had expected, Dusty had formed the correct conclusion on the matter. Not only was the small Texan a courageous fighter and capable leader, but he had a sound business head on his young shoulders. He recognized the significance of supply and demand upon prices.

"There's another market that needs beef," the rancher said and something in his voice warned the listeners that he was approaching the important part of the discussion. "In the East there are whole towns, villages and cities full of folk itching to sink their teeth into beefsteaks, happen the beef's cheap enough for them to buy."

"Mind me asking how we're going to get our cattle to these folks back East, Colonel?" Mark put in. "Are you figuring on trailing them there?"

"Not all the way," Goodnight replied. "My idea is to send them East on the railroad. It's faster and a train'll tote a whole heap more cattle than any boat."

"I'll give you that, Uncle Charlie," Dusty said. "But we're a mite shy on railroads from Texas to the East."

"There's one goes clear across the country, east to west, or will when it's finished," Goodnight pointed out and grinned bleakly as four young mouths began to open. "And, afore any of you smart buttons tell me, I know that railroad's up in Kansas not here in Texas."

"And you figure on trailing the cattle clear up to Kansas, Colonel?" Dawn gasped.

"Why not?" countered Goodnight. "Oliver Loving and I've taken herds nearly as far. But to make it pay, you'll need a whole new conception of trail driving than's been tried so far. Bigger herds, two or three thousand head at least."

Nobody spoke for over a minute after Goodnight completed his statement. Yet he could see that the girl and the three young men were impressed by his comments. Taking his eyes from Goodnight's face, Dusty turned to them to meet Mark's gaze.

Cattle could be gathered and held in bunches at least as large as those mentioned by Goodnight, their herd instincts keeping them together. The question was whether so many half-wild longhorns could be persuaded to go in a desired direction. If so, crazy as it might seem at first hearing, the rancher's scheme had much to commend it. Certainly it offered the answer to the two major problems facing Texas cattlemen: where to sell their stock for a working profit and how to get the animals to the market. Unlike sending the cattle by boat, trailing them would entail no shipping costs other than necessities for the journey, food and pay for the cowhands. The cattle would supply their own transportation to the railroad and, by foraging as they did all their lives on the open range, cut out the high cost of feeding them on the way to the market.

There were, however, objections to Goodnight's scheme.

"Nobody's ever tried to handle a herd that size," Mark said.

"Three thousand head'd take maybe thirty men—" Dusty went on.

"That's something else," Goodnight interrupted. "I figure that we're using too many men on the drives. Once the herd settles in to the trail, eighteen hands at most would be enough."

"*Eighteen!*" Dusty repeated.

"Eighteen, riding point, swing and drag," Goodnight insisted. "I found that out on the last drive. Nine men could handle the fifteen hundred head better than the full crew; they could see what was happening and didn't get in each other's way like when the full bunch were there. Eighteen trail hands, a cook, his louse, one to three men handling the remuda and a scout. If it can be done with just them, making a drive to Kansas'll pay enough to be worth making."

"So that's why you sent for us," Mark breathed. "To help you do it."

"To see if handling three thousand head can be done," the rancher corrected. "We'll be taking along three thousand head, but to Fort Sumner, not Kansas this time." He paused, scanning the faces before him and reading an unspoken question on them. "If I'm so sure we can make it to Kansas, why am I headed for Fort Sumner?"

"The notion did sort of cross my mind," Mark admitted.

"And you've already given the answer. Nobody's tried to handle a herd of three thousand. So I figure it'd be best if we made the first one over a trail I know real well, with good food and water all the way and a certain market at the other end."

"So there might not be a market in Kansas?" Dawn asked, disappointment plain in her voice.

"There's always that chance," Goodnight told her, "although I'm sure the market's there. However, the cost of financing such a drive will be heavy. That's why I'm staking everything I've got on this big drive to Sumner. I'm bonded for every nickel I own to deliver three thousand head to the Fort before July—at eight cents a pound, on the hoof."

"*Eight* cents a pound, on the hoof!" Dawn croaked and even the impassive features of the Ysabel Kid registered emotion. "Why that's—that's—"

Words failed Dawn as she tried to make an estimate of just how much money the completion of the contract would bring to Goodnight. An average steer beyond that age weighed around eight hundred pounds on the hoof. Growth continued and, from ten years until senile decline set in, a steer could go up to one thousand pounds, or in exceptional cases as high as sixteen hundred. Knowing that, Dawn's mind boggled at the thought of what a herd of three thousand head would be worth when delivered to Fort Sumner. One eight-hundred-pound steer would fetch sixty-four dollars and, in a herd that size, there would be many weighing far heavier.

"That's real important money," Dusty finished for her, having followed much the same line of thought.

"More than enough to finance a drive to Kansas," Goodnight agreed. "But only *if* I can fulfill the contract."

"Which you can't without that eleven hundred head Chisum was supposed to bring," Mark guessed.

"That's about the size of it," the rancher agreed.

"Damn it!" Dawn spat out. "I wish I'd never come after them damned critters!"

"Don't feel that way, I'm not blaming you," Goodnight smiled. "They were your cattle and you'd every right to get them back."

"And you've likely saved Uncle Charlie a mess of trouble," Dusty continued. "If he'd not found out in time, those cattle would've been mixed with his herd. I don't reckon the Army'd've too high regard for his honesty if he'd showed up with maybe one in three head carrying somebody else's brand and him not able to prove how he came by them."

"Even if the Army took them, word'd get out," Mark went on. "Folks'd call Colonel Charlie a thief. No rancher takes kindly to being stolen from and they'd like it a whole heap less when they learned how much he was paid for their stock."

"My contract calls for straight brands," Goodnight said quietly. "The Army would cancel if they were faced with a herd of stolen stock.

"Only you'd've found out about the brands before you arrived," Dusty pointed out. "Even if Chisum'd've mixed them in with your herd, you'd've seen some of the brands when you trail counted, or looked the cattle over. But by that time, it'd be too late for you to replace them."

"How bad off does losing that bunch of Chisum's leave you, Colonel?" Mark asked bluntly.

"Bad enough. He's always played straight with me before, so I only gathered around two thousand head of my own. Figured to have my boys building up a herd for Kansas while I was away and making the drive with Chisum's hands."

"Can't you round up enough to fill the contract?" Dusty inquired.

"Not in time. This part of the year, most of the cattle've moved back into the brush country and're harder to move out than borrowing neighbors. Even if we got them, I've only three men without stripping the spread of its work crew."

"When Colin Red and Billy Jack come, we make it up to seven even with Lon riding scout," Dusty said.

"Which still leaves us eleven trail hands short," Goodnight reminded him. "A herd of three thousand couldn't be handled with less than eighteen men."

Much as Dawn wanted to speak, she found herself unable to utter the words which crowded her mouth ready to be uttered.

"I reckon getting the cattle'd be easy enough, Uncle Charlie," Dusty remarked. "If Dawn's pappy and their neighbors can bring in a thousand head, that'll give you the full herd to fill the contract."

"There's the hundred Chisum wide-looped from us for starters," Dawn agreed eagerly. "And most everybody around us've been gathering for when the hide-and-tallow man comes. They'd sooner sell to the Army—"

Her words trailed off as she realized that her father and their neighbors would not be selling to the Army. It seemed highly unlikely that Goodnight would pay eight cents a pound and then drive the cattle to Fort Sumner and only get the same price for them.

"Maybe Dawn could help you get the hands while she's at it," Dusty remarked, guessing what was on the girl's mind.

"We've three of 'em back home, doing nothing but sit on their butt ends most of the time," Dawn admitted. "Trouble being none of 'em's ever been on a long drive."

"Neither have Dusty and the OD Connected boys," Goodnight answered. "That's why they're coming along. Maybe your pappy and some of his neighbors would like to send hands to drive the cattle and learn how it's done."

"They'll be green hands," Mark said.

"And so will the crews that go north to Kansas," Goodnight replied. "So if it comes off, this'll be more than just a trail drive. You know that we've no industries in Texas capable of competing on a national level and no mineral resources to bring money into the State.* All we've got is cattle. But we've got more of them than any other state or territory in this whole country. And we've got the grazing land to keep on raising them. But not if we have to sell out breeding

---

*It would be many years before oil became a factor in the Texas economy.

stock and strip the ranges bare for the hide-and-tallow factories. If we can get to Kansas, we'll have a market for beef and won't need to sell bulls or cows at three dollars a head. Dawn, boys, if we can show that it's possible to trail a big herd, we'll help haul this old State of our'n up by its bootstraps and set it back on its feet."

Then the rancher coughed and his face resumed its usual grim, unemotional lines. He studied the four young faces and saw no derision to his rhetoric. Instead they glowed with enthusiasm.

"You mean you'll take some of our boys along just so they can learn how it's done?" Dawn asked.

"I will," Goodnight agreed. "Then they'll be able to teach others and the money the cattle bring will help finance your drives north."

If Dawn had felt admiration for Goodnight before, it increased in leaps and bounds at his words. Instead of taking advantage of his neighbors, buying their stock cheap and taking it to sell at a vast profit, he was offering to share his good fortune with them. More than that, he appeared willing to let some of them go along to learn the trail and how to handle a large bunch of cattle.

Dusty felt no such surprise at his uncle's generosity. Money meant little to a man like Charles Goodnight. He was willing to throw his experience to the benefit of his neighbors. Once other ranchers saw the trailing of large herds was possible, they could be counted on to make the attempt. Using the countless herds of longhorns which roamed practically unchecked over the Texas ranges, the ranchers would bring badly needed money into the State. Then there could be development, growth, expansion. That was Goodnight's dream. Dusty and the floating outfit had been sent by Ole Devil Hardin to help Goodnight make his dream come true.

TEN

That's Sutherland's *Golondrino*

"Remember, Miss Dawn," Goodnight told the girl as she sat on her *bayo-tigre* gelding ready to start the journey home. "The men your pappy and neighbors pick to come must be here with the cattle in eight days at most."

"We'll be here," the girl promised. "Eleven hundred head, all steers."

"That's it," the rancher agreed. "They travel faster than a mixed herd and steers're what the Army want."

"I'll mind it all," she promised.

Watching the girl's eager face, Goodnight hoped that she was not raising her hopes too high and was doomed for disappointment. A pioneer at the business of long-distance cattle herding, he knew the risks involved and the problems it presented. Even with a smaller herd and trained crew, reaching Fort Sumner was anything but a sinecure. Taking along fifteen men—skilled as they might be at general ranch work—who had never been on an extended journey of that kind multiplied the odds against getting the steers through.

Yet the try must be made and the experience gained by the cowhands would be invaluable on later drives. Given the cooperation of Sutherland and his neighbors, the drive might pave the way for the rest of Goodnight's dream to become a reality.

It was dawn and, despite sitting up late discussing the scheme, the girl was ready to ride home. Mark and the Kid, the former authorized to act as Goodnight's spokesman, were to accompany her. Riding relay, they hoped to make very fast time to her home and make an early start at gathering the cattle. The steers retrieved from Chisum were to be added to Goodnight's shipping herd, for Dawn knew her father would leap at the chance offered by the bearded rancher.

Two hours later, Dusty sat at the side of a small lake. With his left leg hooked up comfortably over the horn of his paint stallion's saddle, he looked around with interest. Scattered before him were numerous specimens of the creature upon which the future of Texas depended. They were two thousand head of longhorn steers gathered and held together by Goodnight's men. Surrounded by plentiful grazing, protected from visitations by predatory animals, with good water close at hand, the steers showed little inclination to roam. Of course the arrival of the D4S cattle—brought from the vicinity of the ranch house by the men coming to handle the herd during the day—could be expected to make the Swinging G stock restless.

Although every bit as much creatures of a herd as American bison, prairie-dogs or pronghorn antelope, the longhorns did not show the other species' uniformity of coloration. Steers of almost every imaginable animal color dotted the land before Dusty. Brindles, duns, dark, washed-out or Jersey creams, bays, browns, reds, blacks, whites, mulberry, ring-streaked or speckled blues, *grullas* the mousy brown shade of sandhill cranes, *golondrinos*, and mixtures of colors almost beyond number or belief.

"That's a fine gather you've made, Uncle Charlie," Dusty commented, turning to where his uncle sat by his side.

"Good enough," the rancher agreed. "Only we'll not be able to hold them here for much more than a week. John Poe allows they were a mite restless last night."

"He reckons it was somebody making them that way?"

"Nope. There were wolves howling off to the south. We'll have to keep them close watched from now on, though. They don't take to being held overlong in one place even on good grazing."

"Given just a smidgen of good Texas luck, Mark'll have Dawn's folk from Mineral Wells in seven days at most. I'll bet that gal doesn't give anybody a lick of peace until she's got the cattle headed here."

"I only hope that—" Goodnight began.

"Colonel Charlie!" a cowhand called and pointed to the east. "Riders coming."

Bringing down his raised foot, Dusty joined his uncle in looking at the approaching men. They were about fifteen in number.

"They're cowhands, mostly," Dusty said, as the men drew closer. "Could be they've heard about Chisum pulling out and're looking for work."

By that time the riders were near enough for

Goodnight to make identifications and he shook his head.

"They're not. That big feller up the front's Tom Wardle, runs the Bench P. Then there's Harry Hultze of the Double Two, Myron Colburn from the Lazy F and Mel Jones of the Flying H. Rest of 'em look like hands from their spreads."

"All of them lost cattle to Chisum," Dusty breathed. "They friends of yours?"

"Not what you'd call close friends," Goodnight admitted. "Tom Wardle was took prisoner by the Yankees in the War and worked up a real hate for them, way he was treated in their prison camp. That hate takes in anybody who didn't ride for the South. Rest of them're his neighbors and go along with his play."

A frown creased Dusty's brow as he turned over Goodnight's words. While a loyal Texan, his uncle had declined to take up arms for the South. Facing the bands of marauding Indians, Mexican *bandidos* or *Comancheros* had been every bit as dangerous as wearing the blue or grey in defense of one's beliefs. Unfortunately, not all who went to war saw it in that light.

There was another point to consider. All of the men had lost cattle which should have been delivered into Goodnight's herd. For some reason they had left the trail of the stolen cattle. That reason could mean trouble for the bearded rancher.

In the lead rode a tall, well-built man wearing a white Jeff Davis campaign hat, open military tunic with a major's star on the collar and the "chicken-guts" insignia of the same rank on its sleeves. Yellow-striped cadet-grey riding breeches and shining boots completed his clothing. A weapon belt of issue design, except that its holster had no top, was cinched about his lean middle. His moustached face was set in grim lines and had the air of expecting obedience about it.

All the others wore range clothes in varying degrees of value. The two tall, lean men and the short, thickset rider immediately behind the military figure had the undefinable look of employees rather than employed. Every member of the party had at least one holstered revolver and several carried rifles across their knees. The latter struck Dusty as being particularly ominous. Men on a peaceful mission, or in search of help, did not approach in such a manner.

At a sign from the military man, most of the party halted and fanned into a fighting line. Followed by the other three ranchers, all darting suspicious glances at the cattle, the leader came toward Goodnight and Dusty.

"Howdy, Tom," Goodnight greeted. "You're a mite off your home range."

"So's some of our cattle," Wardle answered, sitting cavalry-smart in his saddle and looking from Goodnight to Dusty. "Heard tell that John Chisum was bringing you a herd. Did he get it here?"

"Had it outside Graham yesterday," Goodnight admitted.

"Did you check the brands before you took the herd from him?" demanded the lanky Myron Colburn. "See, Colonel Charlie, we've all lost a fair slew of cattle and trailed 'em up this way."

"And you reckon that I might have stolen stock in my herd?" Goodnight asked.

While Wardle regarded anybody who stayed at home during the War as being a Yankee sympathizer, he had never doubted Goodnight's honesty. So he threw an angry glare at his companions, then turned to

Goodnight and shook his head.

"Nobody's accusing you, Charlie," Wardle stated. "Only we heard Chisum was headed this way and came over to see him."

"He's not here," Goodnight told the ranchers. "As soon as I saw the brands on the herd, I knew he didn't own them and told him that I didn't want them."

"Looks like we come up here for nothing," grunted the thickset Hultze. "I told you that we should've stuck to the tracks instead of coming straight here."

While his uncle talked with the ranchers, Dusty studied the rest of the men. All but three looked like ordinary cowhands, tough, capable, loyal to the brands they rode for. The exceptions sat just a shade away from the others. Not much, but sufficient for a man who knew the signs to notice.

Slouching in their saddles, the trio were tall men. One had red hair, surly features and wore a low-hanging Colt while cradling a Spencer carbine across his right arm. The second was black-haired, dark, broken-nosed with cruel eyes and armed like the first. Although his companions might have passed as cowhands, the third man certainly could not. A dirty coonskin cap fitted over long, lank brown hair while his lean face was bristle-stubbled. His grease-blackened buckskin shirt tucked into blue cavalry breeches from which Indian leggings extended to the tops of his moccasins. His belt carried a Navy Colt and a long cavalry sabre. Lying across the crook of his arm was a brass tack-decorated Sharps rifle.

The three men sat listening to the conversation and Dusty noticed that Hultze threw a malevolent scowl their way while making his last comment. As if wanting to avoid further recriminations, the redhead moved his horse forward. Although the second man followed, the buckskin-shirted man continued to sit motionless in the background.

"That's a fair-sized bunch of cattle," the redhead said. "Can we cut it?"

In view of Goodnight's statements, the suggestion bordered on being an insult. Annoyance flickered on Wardle's face and he spoke before the bearded rancher could answer.

"Colonel Goodnight's word is good enough for me."

"Your brand lost at most a hundred head," the redhead answered. "And you wouldn't've missed them yet if I hadn't come by hunting for the stock we had stolen."

"Which ranch's that, mister?" Dusty asked.

Up to then the newcomers had hardly noticed Dusty. His words brought their eyes to him and Wardle in particular studied him with extra interest. However, the redhead merely raked the small Texan with a cold, insolent gaze.

"The name's Luhmere, *boy*. I ride for the Rocking N. Our boss missed a bunch we'd gathered and sent me 'n' Turner here after 'em."

"Just the two of you?" Dusty inquired.

"Who're you, Goodnight's son?"

"His nephew, mister. Your boss must have a whole heap of faith in you."

"How'd you mean?" Luhmere growled.

"Sending just the two of you after a bunch of cow thieves."

"He figured we'd be enough, sonny," Turner put in. "We found where they'd gathered stock from these gents and passed the word about it. Then we come to get whoever was doing the stealing."

"Why come here?" Goodnight asked.

"This's where the tracks pointed," Luhmere replied.

"Only you didn't stick with the tracks," Dusty pointed out.

"That feller Scroggins there met up with us late yesterday afternoon," Wardle explained, indicating the man in the coonskin cap. "He told us that Chisum was trailing in a herd for Colonel Charlie—"

"And damned if it wasn't the same herd that we're tracking," Luhmere interrupted. "So we come straight here, fixing to take our cattle back."

Cold anger flashed into Goodnight's eyes but he held his temper. The nature of the redhead's words formed an insult that might easily result in bloodshed. Other members of Wardle's party saw it in that light. Shifting to more ready positions in their saddles, the cowhands waited for their employers guidance.

Fortunately the ranchers were not hotheads. Wardle might be antagonistic to Goodnight's lack of support for the Confederacy, but he had no desire to meet the other rancher in open conflict. Especially when he suspected that the *big* man on the paint stallion was Captain Dusty Fog, who nobody could claim had failed to give full and complete loyalty to the Confederate States. Having less cause to hate the Yankees, the other ranchers admitted that Goodnight had served Texas well during the War. So they were willing to accept his statement about the cattle as long as Tom Wardle did the same.

"It ain't that ways at all, Charlie," the lanky Jones announced hurriedly. "We allowed you'd do the right thing by us, Charlie, if Chisum'd brought our cattle here, and figured to save time by coming straight over."

Dusty noticed that Luhmere and Turner appeared surprised by the ranchers' lack of activity. Letting out a snort, Luhmere looked at the men who had accompanied him. "Damn it to hell! We come here to get the

Rocking N's steers back and ain't no copperhead Yankee-lover going to stop us."

Still Goodnight did not lose his temper. He saw the tightening of Wardle's lips but spoke before the other rancher could make any statement.

"I've told you that I never had the cattle from Chisum. He took them with him when he left, allowing to turn them loose where he picked them up."

"We didn't meet him," Luhmere pointed out.

"Likely you would have if you'd stuck to the tracks," Goodnight replied.

While the men were talking, a mulberry-colored Swinging G steer let out a bellow. Dropping its head, it charged at one of the D4S animals which approached a particularly succulent piece of grazing. Deciding from experience that discretion was better than valor, the newcomer whirled and fled. When the aggressor did not halt, the D4S steer followed a course which had frequently saved it from attack by its better-armed rivals. Spiking its tail out, it raced through the other cattle and toward the group of riders. It could hardly have picked a worse time to appear.

"Hey!" Colburn barked, stabbing a finger in the fleeing animal's direction. "That's Sutherland's *golon-drino* muley. I'd know it any place. It allus runs to a rider if another steer chases it. Damned near caused a stampede doing it last fall at our roundup."

ELEVEN

We've Done What We Came To Do

"Chisum picked up some of Darby Sutherland's stock!" Hultze ejaculated.

"If Sutherland's steers're here, so's our'n!" Luhmere yelled.

"Damned I don't go take a look!" Turner went on.

Dusty cursed silently as he saw the effect Colburn's words had on the rest of the men from Mineral Wells. Certainly the *golondrino* could hardly have picked a worse moment at which to be chased from the herd. Up to that point, the ranchers had been willing to accept Goodnight's word that he had turned away Chisum and the stolen cattle. Seeing the D4S muley had aroused their suspicions, even without the two hardcases' comments.

All too well Dusty realized what the consequences might be if Luhmere and Turner started to ride forward. Enough of Goodnight's hands were within hearing distance to be aware that something was wrong. So they would intervene, it being considered an insult to cut another man's herd. That could easily bring the rest of the newcomers into the fray. In which case a bloody gunbattle might easily result and, even if the Swinging G came out victorious, the cattle were sure to stampede."

On making for the herd, Luhmere and Turner directed their horses in Dusty's direction. Like others before and after them, they failed to form a correct estimation of the small Texan's full potential. Studying the insignificant figure lounging on the paint, Luhmere concluded that he might be provoked into a reckless attempt at stopping them cutting the herd. Like Dusty, Luhmere understood the danger and figured that it could be exploited to its full advantage.

Leering in a taunting manner, calculated to make an impetuous youngster—eager to prove himself a worthy nephew of Colonel Goodnight—act in a hot-headed manner, Luhmere waited for Dusty's first hostile move. When none came, he swung his horse to pass close on Dusty's right while Turner aimed his horse to go by on the other side.

Slowly Dusty lifted his right hand toward his Stetson, giving the impression that he either meant to mop his brow or push it back and scratch his head. Nothing in the way he moved gave warning of his true purpose, but he was studying every detail and making his plans. Each of the men carried a Spencer carbine cradled across his left arm. While Turner's barrel pointed toward Dusty, that of Luhmere's lined outward and neither weapon's hammer was cocked.

One of the Spencer's failings was that it must be cocked manually before each shot. Dusty figured that the drawing back of the hammer ought to give him just the split-second advantage he needed.

From its slow, hesitant crawl upward, Dusty's hand flashed into the sudden, rapid movement for which he was famous. Twitching off the Stetson, he spun it as hard as he could at Luhmere's face. Instinctively the man jerked himself backward in the saddle and, belatedly, tried to throw up his right hand to deflect the flying hat. In doing so he jerked at his horse's mouth, causing it to rear in protest. With a startled yell, Luhmere felt himself slipping backwards over the cantle of his saddle. Losing his hold on the Spencer as he tried to retain his seat, he fell rump-first to the ground.

After hurling the hat, Dusty gave his attention to the second man. Swiveling in the paint's saddle, he saw Turner starting to thumb back the Spencer's hammer. Even in the urgency of the situation, Dusty did not forget to think. He realized that if he deflected the carbine to his front, he might endanger the lives of the men before him. So he grasped the end of the barrel and turned it to his rear. Once he was no longer in danger, Dusty jerked savagely at the weapon. Just an instant too late, he saw that Turner had acted faster than he expected. The hammer had been taken far enough backward to be operative. Combined with the force of Dusty's pull and his own resistance, Turner squeezed the trigger. With a bellow, the carbine spat out a ball which split the air by the ear of its user's horse and flew on to drive into the ribs of a grazing steer. Letting out an agony-filled bellow, the stricken animal went kicking to the ground. Its companions, already made restless by the wolves during the night and the recent arrival of the D4S steers, needed no other excuse to break and run.

Startled by the close-passing bullet and the heat of the carbine's muzzle-blast, Turner's horse humped its back and took off in a leaping buck. Timing his move perfectly, Dusty gave a harder heave at the carbine and twisted it from Turner's grasp. Struggling to keep astride the horse, Turner lost his balance as the Spencer left his fingers. Pitching out of the saddle, the man crashed to the ground.

At the sight of his cattle stampeding, Goodnight opened his mouth to bellow orders. Starting to rein his horse around, he saw Scroggins begin to lift the Sharps. Down lashed the rancher's right hand, sliding the offside Colt from its holster and getting off a fast shot. Fast or not, it flew in a useful way. Striking the bottom of the rifle's barrel, the bullet batted it from Scroggin's hands; although, it must be confessed, the rancher had not tried for such a spectacular effect. Goodnight continued to turn his horse and, holstering his Colt, sent it leaping after the departing cattle.

To give them their due, the other ranchers showed no hesitation in going to help Goodnight. Even before Dusty could swing his paint into movement, the ranchers and their men urged their horses on Goodnight's heels. Easing his big horse around the unseated Turner, Dusty galloped after the other to lend a hand at stopping the stampede.

Spitting out curses and shaking his stinging hands, Scroggins rode toward the two hardcases.

"I'll get the bas-!" Scroggins swore, snatching at his holstered revolver and glaring rage after Goodnight.

"Forget him and catch our hosses!" yelled Luhmere, getting to his feet and stamping furiously on Dusty's hat. "We'd best get the hell away from here."

"Yeah!" agreed Turner, rising and retrieving his

carbine. "It didn't work like it should have. I thought Wardle was supposed to hate Goodnight's guts."

"And me," Luhmere admitted. "He's got no cause to care for copperheads."

"Looks like he don't count Goodnight that way," Turner growled. "And when him and them others find out that Goodnight spoke the truth, they're going to be wanting to ask us some questions."

Maybe Scroggins could not be rated among the world's great thinkers, but he fully understood what his companions meant. Their motives for bringing the four ranchers to Goodnight's herd would not stand up to close scrutiny. Already cattlemen were building up a reputation for dispensing effective, if not entirely legal, justice to transgressors against their code. So Scroggins wasted no more time and started his wiry horse moving after Luhmere's and Turner's mounts.

"What do we do now, Lou?" Turner inquired. "We've done what we came to do, stampeding Goodnight's herd that way."

"Goodnight's still alive," Luhmere pointed out. "The bosses wanted him dead. We'll see if we can find somewhere to hide out. Then one of us can head up to Throckmorton and see if they want anything more doing while the other two keep an eye on how things're going down here."

"It'd be best," Turner said and walked over to collect Scroggin's rifle.

When the buckskin-clad man returned with the horses, the trio mounted. They saw the herd trailing off in the distance and exchanged grins.

"Stampede!" the Texans called it. Mexicans said, "*Estampida*." Both words meant what the ancient Greek cattle-herders termed "fear-panic" running; trouble, danger, possibly sudden and violent death for the men trying to stop the fleeing cattle.

Once started, the two thousand head of longhorn steers tore across the range at their best speed. Hooves thundered and shook the ground with the fury of their combined impact. Occasionally horns clacked or clicked against each other when two of the racing animals drew close together. Vocal as the longhorn might be at times, it made no sound when running. At such a time every breath of air sucked in was expended on propelling the body onward as fast as the steel-spring power of the leg muscles could carry it. Wild-eyed, heads tossing, tails spiked into the air, the steers raced on in their wild, mindless, unthinking fear.

Small groups broke away from the main bunch, cutting off at angles from the line of the stampede and fleeing for the brush country from which they had been gathered at much cost in sweat, blood and hard work by the Swinging G cowhands.

Cursing, hard-riding men followed the fast-running, disintegrating herd. While some of them tried to reach the lead steers, others attempted to turn back the segments which separated from the main body. In this Wardle's men found themselves at a disadvantage. Going after a bunch of cow thieves called for a horse with "bottom," the ability to travel long and fast, rather than for skill at working cattle. So, for the most part, they sat horses not suited to handling fear-spooked steers. Although they and the Swinging G's hands did their best, a number of the groups escaped and fled.

After saving Dusty from being back-shot by Scroggins, Goodnight gave his full attention to retrieving his herd. Once cattle, especially longhorn steers, started to run in wild stampede, there was considerable danger to themselves and the men trying

to halt them. Unless brought to a halt by their human
guardians, the cattle would run on until stopped by
sheer exhaustion. During that time they would also be
scattered across the range and have worked off every
ounce of spare fat and meat. There was, Goodnight
knew, only one way to end a stampede and he prepared
to attempt it.

The horse he sat was a fourteen-hand *bayo-
cebrunos* gelding of Spanish blood and with genera-
tions of cattle-working savvy behind it. Seeing the
stampede, the gelding needed no urging and little
instruction from its rider on what it would be required
to do.

Before the rancher had returned his right hand to
the reins from holstering his Colt, the *bayo-cebrunos*
started running. Stretching itself at full gallop, the
gelding sped across the range after the fleeing cattle.

Despite the publicity later given to firing revolver
shots alongside the lead steer's head as a means of
turning a herd, it was a method only resorted to in the
direst emergency or by green hands. All too often, it
did no more than spur on and further frighten the herd.
So Goodnight gave no thought to his holstered Colts
and concentrated on guiding the fast-moving *bayo-
cebrunos*.

Experience had taught Goodnight that running
cattle tended to turn to the right more willingly than to
the left. He attributed the trait to the fact that, like
human beings, the majority of animals are "right-
handed" and preferred to turn at speed in the direction
which offered them the greatest strength and control.
Whatever the reason, Goodnight wanted to utilize it as
a means to make his cattle "mill" and so be forced to
stop.

Achieving that intention presented a problem. He

punishment, the steer continued to move away. The *bayo-cebrunos* missed its footing and stumbled. Deftly, with a riding skill a Comanche would have admired, Goodnight adjusted his balance to assist it. For a moment the rancher wondered if it was his finish. Then the horse regained its footing and plunged in to let him slam another kick at the steer.

Close behind Goodnight, Wardle watched in silent admiration. In the way of their kind, the steers following the ring-streaked blue swung after it as it turned and Wardle was ready to prevent any attempt to deviate from the curve started by Goodnight's kicks. All along the left side of the herd, men prepared to ensure there was no breakaway from the course forced upon its leader.

Unlike his uncle, Dusty had gone along the right flank. The big paint had carried him toward the point but he knew that he could do little to help and so had not caught up to the lead steer. With the other men on the right side, he had given his efforts to holding back hopeful strays. Watching Goodnight turn the ring-streaked blue, Dusty was aware of the danger to the men on his side of the herd.

From a straight line the stampede slowly began to form a circle. The cowhands on the inner flank whirled their horses to ride clear. Last to go was Dusty. After all the others had ridden out, he sent his paint running for the rapidly narrowing gap between the point and drag. He timed the departure just right, having ensured that none of the hands were trapped in the ring and leaving himself before the lead steer came close enough to take fright at his sudden appearance. Once beyond the cattle, he reined the paint around and waited to see if there was anything more he could do.

Instead of allowing the blue steer to join behind the

drag and make a complete circle, Goodnight forced it to turn inwards before it reached the last of the cattle. Once again the others followed their leader, passing along the right flank and forming an ever-decreasing spiral. The cowhands did their best to keep the cattle moving, causing them to mill closer and closer until the big blue found itself unable to continue forward due to the pressure of the others around it. In that way the movement of the herd was brought to a halt.

"Circle them, keep them held!" Goodnight yelled to the cowhands.

There might still be danger if some of the steers broke out of the tight-packed mass. However, the worst of the trouble was over and the rancher could withdraw to try to assess what losses he had suffered through the stampede.

"Thanks, Tom, boys," he said as the other ranchers rode toward him.

"You'd've done the same for any of us, Charlie," Wardle replied. "Our boys'll tend to the herd. You send your crew off to see what they can gather from the strays."

Nodding gratefully, Goodnight turned to give the orders. He knew that the stampede had caused a serious loss of stock. Just looking at the packed-together mass of the remainder told him that. Just how bad the losses would be, he could not tell for certain; but he estimated well over five hundred steers had broken away. A few would be dead, others picked up and returned by his men. The majority of the escapees were headed back to the brush country as fast as their legs could carry them. Even if the Mineral Wells men accepted his offer, it looked like he would still be a lot of cattle short of the number required to fulfil his contract with the Army.

TWELVE

Listen To The Blood Call

"Bad, huh?" Wardle said sympathetically, following the direction of Goodnight's gaze.

"It could've been a whole heap worse," the bearded rancher replied. "About that *golondrino*. It was part of a bunch Pitzer Chisum brought in with your stock. Dawn Sutherland had trailed them up here. It was her who first put me wise to Chisum's game. Dustine helped me cut the herd and we took out all the D4S critters. Only she left them with me while she headed for home to see her pappy."

"Ain't that Dawn the spunky one," grinned Jones. "We didn't go to the D4S with Darby having that bust leg. Figured to fetch his stuff back without bothering him. Only young Dawn licked us to it."

"Trust her for that," grinned Hultze. "What happened to our stock?"

"Chisum took it with him," Goodnight replied. "Allowed he'd turn it loose close to its home range. I couldn't've got it without shooting, which'd've spooked the herd anyways."

"We'll tend to his needings," Wardle promised grimly.

Before any more could be said, Dusty rode up.

"I'm real sorry I started the shooting, Uncle Charlie," Dusty said.

"*You* didn't start it," Goodnight corrected.

"I wanted to stop those two yahoos busting through until you'd had time to tell these gents about Dawn Suth—"

"They know now. And my boys wouldn't've let them go into the herd."

"Say. Where the hell're them two jaspers at?" Colburn demanded, rising in his stirrups and staring around. "They could've easy got somebody killed, acting that ways."

"That's what they was after doing, I'd say," Dusty put in as the other ranchers also looked around without locating Luhmere and Turner. "And it was three of them, not two."

"How do you figure that out, Cap'n Fog?" asked Wardle.

"Way I see it, that lanky cuss in the coonskin cap was in it up to his dirty neck," Dusty replied. "And I'll be tolerably surprised if either of the others ride for the Lazy N."

"Comes to that," Colburn remarked. "I know Needles of the Lazy N, and I've never seed either of them fellers on his place."

"Unless things're better for Needles than most of

us," Wardle commented, "I can't seeing him having the money to take on extra help."

"I didn't give much thought to it at the time," Colburn answered. "Hell! When somebody rides in to say you've had your gather wide-looped, you don't stand around asking questions."

"That's for sure," Dusty agreed.

The ranchers dismounted to cool and rest their horses. While waiting, Wardle inquired, "Why'd you reckon Scroggins's in cahoots with Luhmere and Turner, Cap'n Fog?"

"He didn't meet up with us until last night," Hultze went on.

"Way I see it, this all ties in to a play at stopping Uncle Charlie taking his cattle to Fort Sumner," Dusty replied. "First they get to Chisum and persuade him to grab off your stock to replace that herd Pitzer lost. Then they have Luhmere and Turner telling you about the thefts and bringing you after whoever took your cattle. To make sure nothing went wrong, they had Scroggins hid out. He come to you on the trail after dark and said how he'd seen Chisum delivering cattle to Uncle Charlie, likely steered you here—"

"He did," Wardle confirmed.

"They knew you don't like Yankees, Tom," Dusty went on, "and were counting on you regarding Uncle Charlie as one. When you didn't bust in and start the shooting, Luhmere and Turner made a stab at doing it. That damned fool *golondrino* coming out gave them an excuse. Once the first shot'd been fired, you'd've cut in figuring Uncle Charlie was lying about sending your cattle back."

"I'd say they picked on you, figuring you'd make some *loco* move and they could handle you easy, Cap'n Fog," Jones remarked. "If you know what I mean?"

Dusty grinned at the worried expression on the gangling rancher's face. It had been many years since the small Texan's lack of inches had caused him either embarrassment or resentment.

"There's not many'd've thought their game out as quick as you did, Cap'n Fog," Hultze complimented. "Or gone at it the way you did to stop them."

"It was a fool way," Dusty grunted. "Turner moved faster than I expected to cock his Spencer and got off a shot."

"It turned out all right, boy," Goodnight assured him. "Damn it, though, Dawn's flogging hell out of her horse to get back home and see you gents."

"How come?" asked Wardle.

"That's something we could talk over better at the house," Goodnight replied. "If you gents can spare the time to take a meal and a drink, that is."

"We ought to be getting back and cutting Chisum's sign," Jones said. "Time enough for it after we've taken Charlie up on his offer, though."

"If Cap'n Fog's called the play right," Wardle continued, in a tone which showed that he did not doubt it, "Chisum's done what he intended with the herd and'll turn it loose. If I know those steers of mine, they'll find their way back to their home range in the end."

While waiting for the horses to recover from their strenuous exertions, the ranchers saw some of the cowhands returning. A few brought back cattle, but others came in empty-handed with tales of steers fleeing into the bush.

"I went in after a bunch," the young cowhand, Austin, declared, his shirt torn to shreds and his face and torso sporting numerous vicious-looking scratches. "Was following a rattlesnake down a path that got narrower all the time. Only when that old rattler started *backing* out of it, I figured that track was just a touch too tight for me to go along any more."

Knowing the manner in which brush-reared long-horns could pass through dense, almost impenetrable undergrowth, none of the listeners blamed him for failing to bring back the cattle. All the other Swinging G hands knew that they would most likely soon be brush-popping in an attempt to regather the lost cattle and bring the herd to its original strength.

Satisfied that the horses had recovered, the men started to move the herd back to the area from which they had fled. Tired by the stampede, the steers raised no further objections and went quietly. Looking back, Goodnight let out a low sigh of relief. They had come within a hundred yards of the thick country before he managed to turn the lead steer and he knew just how fortunate he had been.

Soon after moving the herd out, Goodnight asked for help to make a trail count. Accompanied by Wardle, he rode ahead.

Concern grew more apparent on Goodnight's bearded face as he watched the last of the steers drawing ever nearer; but the numbers were falling short of the original two thousand. At least three-quarters of the herd had gone by before the count reached one thousand.

Wardle also counted, doing his work thoroughly although he was human enough to take notice of the brands. Seeing only Swinging G and D4S steers, he was fully satisfied that Goodnight had told the truth. The idea that maybe all his own and his companions' stock had been with the herd, but escaped, never entered his head. He was waiting with some eagerness to hear what the other rancher had to discuss.

At last the drag of the herd passed between the two ranchers. Tallying up their count, Goodnight and Wardle came together.

"I make it fourteen hundred and sixty-five, Charlie," Wardle announced.

"And me," Goodnight replied, knowing the number to be correct—and a whole lot short of the two thousand head he needed to finance his dream.

On the point of the herd, the first of the cattle drew near a victim of the stampede. Halting, the leader snuffled at the air. Then it cut loose with an eerie, mournful bellowing. Many of the following animals took up the sound, gathering around the gory body to paw in the earth and hook at the carcass with savage thrusts.

"Listen to the blood call!" Jones said to Dusty as they rode toward the point. "Of all the noises a longhorn, or any other critter, can make, there's nothing sounds worse."

"That's for sure," agreed Hultze who was with them. "I've seen 'em gather off the range and bawl all night around a fresh-stripped hide that the cook'd left hanging on a corral fence."

Dusty took little part in the conversation. The small Texan found his thoughts returning to the other two's comments on the "blood call." Despite having witnessed the phenomenon on the OD Connected range and occasionally during his travels, he had given it little attention. He did not know what quirk of nature, or primeval urge, caused the longhorn cattle to behave in such a manner. Certainly neither sympathy nor solicitude prompted it, for the cattle would hook at and try to gore to death any badly wounded member of the herd. Whatever the cause, Dusty wondered if the "blood call" might be utilized to help rebuild the scattered shipping herd.

As Dusty had said, he came from open-range country. Yet he was all too aware of what rounding up cattle in thick brush meant. If they hoped to gather sufficient steers to cover the stampede's losses, something quicker than the conventional methods must be tried. So Dusty rode along, half listening to the two ranchers as they talked of the cattle industry's troubles or the evils of Reconstruction. All the time he was formulating a plan and hoped for a chance to discuss it with his uncle.

Unsure of whether his idea would work, Dusty wanted to sound Goodnight out in private but there was always somebody close to the rancher. On reaching the lake, Dusty collected his dilapidated hat. Looking at it, he grinned and decided that he was lucky in not having bought a new Stetson the previous afternoon in Graham. No opportunity presented itself to speak to Goodnight while riding from the lake to the ranch house. Approaching the buildings, Dusty found that the remaining members of the floating outfit had arrived and were walking towards him.

Red Blaze was a tall, well-built youngster, Dusty's age, with an untidy mop of flaming red hair and a freckled, pugnaciously handsome face. Dressed in range clothes, he carried twin walnut-handled Army Colts butt forward in twist-hand draw holsters. During the War he had been Dusty's second-in-command and won a reputation for recklessness which somewhat obscured his true virtues. Sure Red managed to find himself in any fight taking place close by, but once involved he became cool and capable. Dusty never hesitated to trust Red in any matter he understood.

Few people, seeing the gangling length, prominent adam's apple and mournful features, would take Billy Jack for a bone-tough, shrewd and efficient cowhand. Dusty knew him to be all of that, and also a reliant sergeant major who had given loyalty and backing on numerous missions against the Yankees in Arkansas. Billy Jack equaled Red in height, but looked like a starving bean pole. However, he could handle his low-hanging Army Colts with precision and accuracy.

"I'm right pleased to see you pair," Dusty greeted.

"That means there's something danged risky to be done," Billy Jack wailed, face contorting into even more woe-filled lines. "You see if it don't, Red. He's likely got them other two varmints killed off already."

"Where's Mark and Lon at, Cousin Dusty?" Red inquired, harboring much the same suspicions as his companion, although on a less drastic level. Then he noticed something else. "Hey! What in hell's happened to your hat?"

Nothing Dusty could do had managed to return the battered Stetson to its former shape. So he had carried it along hanging by its storm-strap from the saddle horn.

"A feller stomped on it," Dusty explained sketchily.

"Same feller's put the bullet through it?" asked Red.

"Nope," Dusty answered. "That was somebody else."

"Now me," declaimed Billy Jack with mournful satisfaction, "I don't have even *one* feller riled at me."

"Damned if I know why," Red grinned, then became seriously hopeful. "Do we have trouble, Cousin Dusty?"

"Some," the small Texan admitted.

While unsaddling the paint, Dusty told Red and

Billy Jack all that had happened since his arrival in Young County.

"That damned Chisum!" Red growled. "We should take out after him—"

"Chisum's only part of the game," Dusty interrupted. "Likely he only went along with it because Pitzer lost that herd and he wanted to make some easy money. Unless I call it wrong, Chisum's out of the deal now. Likely the fellers who used him won't give up that easy. They damned near brought off their play today. And still might unless we can fetch at least five hundred steers out of the brush in the next few days."

"I told you so!" Billy Jack announced dismally, turning to Red. "I said there was something risky a-foot."

"Yeah," agreed Red.

"Dustine, Charles," Goodnight called.

"Yes, sir?" Dusty answered and Red turned on hearing his seldom-used name.

"These gents will be dining with me. Will you tell Rowdy to make the arrangements?"

"Yo!" Dusty replied and let his paint enter the corral. "We'll do it now."

"I dearly love brush-popping," Billy Jack stated as he walked with the other two toward the cook-shack. "Effen a thorn don't gouge your eyes out, the branches bust your ribs, or gut your hoss so it falls and rolls on top of you. And that's only in *thin* brush."

"Young County's different, though," Red informed him. "They don't have wait-a-minute thorns up here—"

"Naw," answered Billy Jack, stoutly refusing to be comforted. "They have wait-a-son-of-a-bitching-hour thorns in this no-account section."

"I figured you boys'd fight shy when it comes to hard work," Dusty put in. "So I thought up a fool notion that might just save us having to go in after them."

Billy Jack let out an explosive snort which expressed disbelief at Dusty thinking out ways to make his life easier.

"Been thinking, Cousin Dusty," the redhead said. "Could be them jaspers who started the stampede're still around and looking for another chance to make fuss for Uncle Charlie."

"Could be," Dusty agreed. "Only, afore you ask, you're not taking out to look for them. I need you and Billy Jack to help me try out this notion of mine."

By that time, they had reached the cook-shack and entered to find John Poe talking with Rowdy. Just awake, the segundo of the Swinging G wore a red undershirt, levis pants and moccasins. Looking at the battered condition of the hat in Dusty's hand, Poe grinned and said:

"Man'd say you've been mixed in some fuss, Dusty."

"Some," Dusty admitted and told about the stampede.

"Damn it!" Poe spat out. "We'll play hell trying to get that five hundred head back again."

Even given such an opportunity, Dusty hesitated before mentioning his idea to the more-experienced Poe. While not sycophants in any way, Red and Billy Jack had become so used to his "fool notions" paying dividends that they expected it to happen. For all his comments on brush-popping, Billy Jack had done little of the work.

On the other hand, Poe had been reared in brush country and could form a far better estimation than the

OD Connected men of the scheme's possibilities. Considering the novel nature of the suggestion he aimed to put out, Dusty wondered if he might be laying himself wide open for ridicule by making it.

"What're you looking so joyful about?" Rowdy inquired, eyeing Billy Jack suspiciously.

"Was thinking," the doleful one answered. "Cap'n Fog ain't telled you the best of it yet."

"What'd that be, Cap'n?" asked the cook.

"Uncle Charlie's entertaining four ranchers, Red and me to dinner at the house tonight," Dusty told him.

"They've got ten men with them," Red went on. "And all of 'em look hungry."

"If they ain't, my cook'll help 'em get that way," Rowdy replied. "Damn it, though, I'm going to need some more meat. How's about getting somebody to go out and butcher a steer for me, John?"

"You've got two of Rio Hondo County's best butchers waiting here, all hot and eager to volunteer."

"Who else's here, Red?" Billy Jack inquired, looking around.

The cook's words had acted as a spring to set Dusty in motion. It almost seemed to be a sign that Rowdy's need for meat came at such a moment. Certainly the cook's requirements came at a time to merge with the small Texan's. So Dusty told Red and Billy Jack what he wanted them to do while demonstrating their talents as Rio Hondo County's two best butchers.

"So that's how it's going to be done," Red commented.

"If it ain't, we've done some messy work for nothing," Billy Jack continued.

Ignoring his companions, Dusty turned to Poe and

explained his idea. Poe stood for a moment deep in thought.

"It could come off," Poe said at last. "How many men do you need, Dusty?"

"I reckon for the first time you and me, with this pair to do the toting that doesn't call for brain-work."

"He means Red and me," Billy Jack soberly informed Poe.

"I'd never've guessed," the foreman sniffed. "When do we start, Dusty?"

"After we've ate," Dusty answered. "With just a smidgen of luck, we'll know if it's going to work and be back here before Uncle Charlie needs us."

THIRTEEN

It's The Damnedest Thing
I Ever Saw

In the Swinging G's main house, the meal was accounted a success by the visiting Mineral Wells ranchers. No business was talked until after the table had finally been cleared. Before their uncle tackled his guests, Dusty and Red excused themselves and left the house.

With his two nephews out of the room, Goodnight raised the subject the other ranchers were waiting to hear. On hearing Goodnight's proposal's, Wardle, Hultze, Jones and Colburn expressed their gratitude and eagerness to go along with him. More than that, Wardle made a formal apology for his past comments about Goodnight's nonparticipation in the War. From that moment everything went exactly as the bearded rancher wanted. Each ranch would supply two of its cowhands, their horses and up to three hundred head of steers. That number would give Goodnight more than he needed to fill the contract, but left a margin for losses on the way. The expenses for the drive were to be shared in proportion to the number of cattle sent. At eight cents a pound on the hoof, even three hundred head would bring to their owner more money than he had seen at one time for many years. So the four ranchers knew they were getting a very good deal. In addition to giving freely of his experience, Goodnight would be providing the cook, his louse, the scout and horse wranglers. It was, as Wardle stated, a most generous offer.

"I don't reckon we'd best go along though," Wardle went on. "Too many chiefs in a war party's bad medicine, so a wise old Comanche once told me."

"What'd be best, I reckon," Colburn remarked "is that we send along two of our best hands, only let them know that they're under Charlie's orders. They'll learn about handling a big herd on the trail and be able to show the rest of us when they get back."

"While they're gone we can be rounding up stock to go to Kansas," Jones continued. "Hey though! If Chisum knows what the Army's paying, he might take our steers to Fort Sumner and sell them for hisself."

"We should maybe get after him!" Hultze growled.

"You could," Goodnight agreed. "Only wouldn't it be better for you to high-tail it for your homes come morning, get your cattle here and go all out to lick him to Fort Sumner?"

"Reckon you can do it, Charlie?" asked Jones.

"He won't take just eight hundred head," Goodnight guessed. "Which means that he'll have to gather more, either on the range or from the Long Rail.

That'll take time. So we stand a good chance of beating him. And when he gets there, your boys will be on hand to claim any stock he's got carrying your brands."

Clearly the idea appealed to his audience's sense of justice. Letting out a whoop of laughter, Colburn slapped his hand on the table top. "Damned if it's not worth risking them steers on the chance of seeing Chisum's face when we do it."

"You'll have the backing to pull it off, anyways," Wardle went on enthusiastically. "Having Cap'n Fog and John Poe along, and all."

"John won't be going. He's needed here to gather more stock to be trailed to Kansas," Goodnight pointed out. "But I'll have Dustine as my segundo on the drive."

None of the men objected to the arrangement and after some more talk about the drive they changed to other topics. Excusing himself, Goodnight left the room.

"Where's Cap'n Fog and John Poe?" he asked a passing cowhand.

"They rode out a piece back," the cowboy answered.

"What for?"

"I dunno. John come to the bunkhouse, put his hat, boots and gunbelt on, took his saddle and lit out with Cap'n Dusty, Red Blaze 'n' Billy Jack."

"Going into town?"

"Didn't head that way."

"Blast 'em!" Goodnight growled. "I wanted to fix up with them about starting the roundup tomorrow so's we can get to it early in the morning."

"Likely they'll be back," the cowboy answered philosophically.

If Goodnight could have seen his nephews, segundo and Billy Jack making their preparations or riding across the range, he would have been even more puzzled. Not that he worried about their absence, figuring that they had good reason for going.

With his Stetson tilted at the correct "jack-deuce" angle over the right eye, spur-carrying boots and low-hanging Army Colt, Poe looked ready for anything and rode a dark bay gelding noted for its skill as a cattle-handler. Dusty sat astride a small but well-made buckskin belonging to his OD Connected mount and brought along by Red and Billy Jack. The latter pair had also selected horses packed with cow-savvy from their mounts. Across Red's saddle hung a cow's freshly removed hide. A wooden bucket, with a tight, secure cover on it, dangled from Billy Jack's saddle horn and he commented bitterly every time it banged against his leg.

"Hope you didn't mind us butchering the cow John," Red remarked, for none of them took the slightest notice of Billy Jack's complaining. "It'd got a bad cut in its leg and we figured it'd be better dead."

"Any steers you'd've found, we could use in the herd," Poe answered. "Even if Dusty's notion works."

"You figure it won't work?" Dusty inquired.

"I'm hoping like hell it does," the Swinging G's segundo stated fervently. "It's sure a novel idea."

On arrival at the herd's bed-ground, Poe warned the night guard to keep an extra careful watch during the hours of darkness. With the steers tired after their wild stampede, there would be little trouble from them. What Poe feared was a further attempt to scatter the cattle. After giving his orders, he pointed out twenty of the steers which were cut from their companions. He made his selection with care, picking with the ease of long practice. Among the selected score was a large ten-year-old, wide-horned animal with a dark brown body and black head and shoulders. Dusty and the two

OD Connected men were to come to know that particular steer very well in the near future.*

"All of 'em's quiet and've been living on the home ranges," the foreman explained to his three companions. "I'd reckon Antelope Ridge'd be a good place for us to try first. The wind'll be right for us and it's clear of where the bunch-quitters'll've gone."

"It's your range, John," Dusty answered, knowing that such local details were beyond him. "Let's get them moving."

"Reckon we'll get done before night," Billy Jack inquired.

"The best we can hope for is to make a start tonight," Poe answered.

Even that hope did not materialize. By the time they drew near to the Antelope Ridge area, the sun hung just at the lip of the western horizon. So they knew that they could not hope to put Dusty's scheme into operation that day.

Making camp about half a mile from their destination, Dusty left Red and Billy Jack to bed down the cattle while he accompanied Poe on an examination of the area selected. From what Dusty saw, conditions there would be ideally favorable to his plan. Satisfied, he and Poe returned to their companions.

"It's all we want," Dusty announced. "There's open ground before the thick brush starts, but enough places for us to hide in while we're waiting."

"Likely it'll rain, or the wind'll change," Billy Jack commented dolefully. "Something'll go wrong for sure."

"Maybe you'll die of the miseries in the night," Red suggested.

"I ain't that lucky," Billy Jack answered, refusing to

*Told in *From Hide and Horn.*

take comfort. "I'll just have to go on and on the way I am."

Despite the lanky cowhand's gloomy predictions, the night passed uneventfully and without any significant change in the weather conditions. Toward dawn, the men left their blankets and made a cold breakfast, for a fire would definitely ruin any hope of Dusty's scheme working. With the food finished, they gathered the cow's hide and bucket, then moved off on foot. Advancing cautiously toward the brush-covered side of Antelope Ridge, Dusty brought the men to a halt by a large rock about a hundred yards from the edge of the dense undergrowth.

"Here'll do," the small Texan told them, feeling the wind blowing from behind him and toward the slope. "Spread the hide on this rock, Cousin Red."

Taking the hide, Red draped it with its hair inward on the rock. Although it had dried out a little, it was still slick with blood from its removal. Stepping aside, Red allowed Billy Jack to bring up the bucket.

"The hired help get all the worse chores," the lanky cowhand moaned as he removed the cover from the bucket.

"That's what us rich folk have hired help for," Dusty informed him.

Making a sour face at the odor which rose to his nostrils, Billy Jack tossed the cover aside and started to raise the bucket. A red stream of blood oozed out as Billy Jack tipped the bucket, spreading itself over the hide before forming a pool on the ground.

"Now let's get the cattle," Poe said, showing what for him was remarkable eagerness.

Returning to their comfortless camp, the four men saddled their horses and rode to where the twenty head brought from the herd were still resting. Although the steers showed some reluctance at leaving their bedground, they gave no sign of trying to escape. That was where Poe's local knowledge had been so invaluable. He knew the cattle in the herd and had selected animals that were born and grew on the open ranges of the Swinging G. So they had no desire to plunge into the black chaparral, *guajilla* and *granjeno* thickets of the slope.

Keeping the steers moving slowly, Dusty and the other riders watched them approaching the hide-draped rock. Red suddenly became aware that his hands were crushing hard on the reins, while Billy Jack was almost holding his breath and forgot to complain. Even Poe exhibited anticipation and excitement. Only Dusty retained an air of complete calm, for all that he was seething inside. The next few minutes would be vital to his idea.

At last the big brown and black steer approached the rock. Pausing for a moment, which seemed to last for hours to the watching men, it sniffed the air. Then it went closer, nostrils quivering as it sucked in the odor of blood and green hide.

"Cut loose, blast you!" Red breathed. "Damn it, let's hear you."

Almost as if it heard, understood the words and was willing to comply, the steer tilted back its head and let out the dolorous notes of the blood call. More of the assembled longhorns caught the smell of death and gathered around the rock. Some of them pawed at the gory earth, others tilted their heads skyward and joined in their leader's mournful bawling.

"It's working!" Billy Jack enthused, dropping his pose for a moment and making an effort to recover it. "I'll bet there ain't any cattle close enough to hear them, though."

"It could be," Dusty admitted. "In which case, you'll have to butcher another cow and we'll try some other place. Come on, let's get hid and wait to see what happens."

During his examination of the area, Dusty had picked out places of concealment for his party. Leaving the cattle about the bloody hide, they split up and went to the points he had allotted to them. Taking cover, they dismounted and prepared for a long wait to see whether the rest of Dusty's scheme would pay. Dusty thought that it might. Even as he swung from the buckskin's saddle, he heard cattle in the brush echoing the eerie sound of the blood call.

On the right side of what Dusty hoped would be the trap, there was only one piece of cover large enough to conceal the waiting men. So he and Poe stood behind the same clump of cat-claw bushes. Beyond the steers, about fifty yards from where Dusty hid, Red stood behind a large rock. Billy Jack was in a hollow, shielded from sight by a growth of *granjeno*.

A few minutes ticked by, then Dusty saw the first of the longhorns emerge from the brush. Loping into view, it headed for the rock and had barely arrived before more cattle left cover.

Slowly the sun started to creep above the eastern rims and the darkness faded away. Yet the blood call continued to vibrate miserably across the range, growing in volume as other longhorns gathered to investigate. They came from the thorny thickets, or trotting across the open land, animals in every stage of development, all drawn as if by a magnet.

Wild excitement filled the cattle. Driven by their frantic eagerness, they thrust and pushed at each other in attempts to reach the center of the crowd. Pawing or tearing at the ground, some of them sent the blood-soaked earth flying into the air. Others reared, almost climbing over their more fortunate companions as they tried to get closer. On the fringes of the growing crowd, cows, calves or steers too light to force their way into the crush, circled around and bawled out bitter protests at being so deprived.

Concealed in their places behind the cat-claw bushes, Dusty and Poe looked at the scene. A growing sense of elation wore away the awe which filled them at what they had started. Poe could not help wondering why the hell nobody had previously thought of using the blood call as a means of gathering cattle.

"It's the damnedest thing I ever saw, Dusty!" Poe breathed. "You've come up with the right answer."

"I sure hope so," Dusty replied. "I'll bet Uncle Charlie's set to roast our hides for not telling him what we planned to do, or that we'd be away all night."

"He'll not worry about that when he sees what we've gathered," Poe guessed. "Damn it, there're *ladinos* coming out of the brush that we've never managed to catch again since they were de-prided and turned loose."

That was a factor of major importance to Poe. The *ladinos* were outlaw cattle smart enough to realize that the thickly grown thorn brush country offered them immunity against their human enemies. So they moved in, adapting to a way of life far removed from that of their open-range kin. Such creatures developed the survival instincts of much-hunted whitetail deer. Normally they were so acutely cautious that they only crept out to graze on the open country during the hours of darkness. Only the attraction of the blood call drew them out and sufficiently lulled their senses to make catching them remotely possible.

"What do you reckon, John?" Dusty whispered after almost an hour.

Studying the longhorns which were still milling, pushing and shoving about the rock, Poe tried to listen to the sounds rising from the brush. Deep in the thorn thickets, more cattle sounded their answers to the mournful racket of those already on the scene. However, the sounds came from far away. There were other factors to be balanced against waiting for the distant callers to gather.

"I'd say we take what we've got, Dusty," the foreman decided. "There're over a hundred head out there and, with luck, at least half of them'll be steers. If we wait, we may lose them."

"That's what I figure," Dusty admitted. "I'll let Red and Billy Jack know to get ready."

While Poe went to his patiently waiting horse, Dusty cautiously inched himself into sight of the other two. He attracted their attention and they withdrew to collect their mounts.

After tightening the girths and making everything ready, Dusty swung astride the buckskin. He unstrapped the forty-foot-long, hard-plaited Manila rope from the saddle horn. Before he offered to ride out, he prepared the rope for use. His right hand gripped just under the honda—the spliced, leather-coated eyelet in the business end of the rope—and gave a few jerks forward. Doing so caused the noose to open out to a usable size, ready for throwing.

Exchanging a nod with Poe, Dusty set off to reap the harvest of his idea. The hide and blood of the butchered cow had brought a number of cattle together around the rock and still held their attention. Yet all still might come to nothing. A premature or awkward appearance by the men might send most of the assembled longhorns racing for safety.

With that in mind, the men stretched forward alongside the necks of their horses and hoped that doing so would delay the moment when the cattle recognized them for what they were. They also held their mounts to a steady, aimless-seeming walk instead of dashing into sight. Wanting to make their net as tight as possible, Red and Poe made for the rock while the other two kept to the fringe of the brush.

Carefully, without hurry, noise or commotion, the men converged on the cattle. A slight movement in the brush caught Dusty's eye. Turning his head, he saw the face of a cougar peering from among the undergrowth. Attracted by the sounds of the cattle and scent of blood, the mountain lion had stalked up in the hope of snatching a meal. With the wind blowing toward it, its scent had not reached the longhorns around the rock. Finding itself observed, the big cat turned and faded away silently.

Already the blood spilled on the ground had been horn-hooked and hoof-churned almost into oblivion and the bloody hide was losing most of its attraction. Fortunately, by that time the tamer steers brought as decoys from the herd had been forced, or had moved voluntarily, to the edge of the assembly. Being used to the sight of men, they raised no alarm over the approaching riders.

Aided by the same steers, the four men started the cattle moving. Not until a half mile or more separated them from the brush did the first of the *ladinos* begin to realize their danger. If the awareness had come simultaneously, all might been lost. Luckily the in-born herd instincts dulled the *ladino*'s perceptions. Taking comfort from the company of their kind, they allowed themselves to be hazed farther and farther from safety.

Then one of the steers became aware of what was happening. Twisting out of the gather, it tried to escape. At a signal, Dusty's buckskin sprang to head off the bunch-quitter. Coming alive in the small Texan's hands, the rope flew through the air. Finding its fore feet suddenly trapped, the *ladino* crashed to the ground with some force. On rising dazedly, after being freed from the encircling noose, the animal went willingly to rejoin its companions.

That was not the only attempt at flight. If the animal making it was a cow, bull or too young for their purposes, it would be allowed to go. Not so any steer. When one suitable for shipment tried to escape, it found its efforts frustrated by a fast-riding man with a well-trained horse and a rope which seemed almost a living being eager to obey its user's will and enforce his demands. Even the most ardent brush-popping *ladino* needed only to be busted to the ground once with a fore-foot catch* to learn the wisdom of obedience.

At last the shipping herd came into sight. Any indication Goodnight might have felt at his nephew's and segundo's absence died when he saw what they brought with them. Riding to meet them, he recognized several notorious *ladinos* among the cattle and figured one of the quartet had come up with a mighty smart notion for solving his problem of replacing the stock lost in the stampede.

"Well," Red said in a challenging manner as he let Billy Jack come alongside him. "It didn't rain, the wind didn't change and we got 'em here without losing a single steer."

*Described in *Trail Boss*.

"I'll bet they all die off with the 'big jaw,'" the lanky cowhand replied.

It took a lot to make Billy Jack give up and look at the bright side of life.

THIRTEEN

It's The Damnedest Thing I Ever Saw

Faced with proof that Dusty's "fool notion" worked, Goodnight did not hesitate to put it to further use. In the days while Wardle, Jones, Colburn and Hultze returned to Mineral Wells, gathered their steers and got them headed toward Young County, the Swinging G men placed out hides, poured blood on the ground and learned much about utilizing the blood call as a means of rounding up cattle. Goodnight saw the size of the shipping herd grow far faster than it would have by any conventional method he might have tried.

Not all the attempts were as successful as the first. There had been times when the gory earth and bloody hide evoked no response; or the blood call from the reliable, decoy steers failed to produce any of their wilder kin. Experiments taught the men that, from their point of view, the blood and hide of a cow had a better effect than that of a bull or steer. Once an ever-excited Austin forgot his orders and lost them what would have been a good gather by bursting out of concealment recklessly and spooking the longhorns. Another time, a poorly positioned cowhand—it was Loving's companion, Spat—was spotted by a wily old *ladino*, which cut loose with a shattering bellow of warning as it fled and frightened off other cattle headed for the bloody hide.

Yet there had also been times when all went well. Sufficient of them, in fact, for the herd to regain its original members by the fifth day after the Mineral Wells ranchers' departure. Of course there were flurries of activity when determined efforts were made by individual steers or groups to escape; but for the most part they settled into their new environment in a satisfactory manner.

While the cowhands gathered cattle, Rowdy and his louse attended to collecting food and supplies for the six-hundred-mile journey or saw to it that the two wagons were in perfect working condition. The two wranglers and night hawk who would handle the sixty-strong remuda went over every horse, learning the habits of as many of them as possible and making sure all kept in the best of health. For three days the local blacksmith, helped by Billy Jack and one of Goodnight's men, made up and fitted cold shoes to the horses. These, known as "good-enoughs," would be carried in barrels on the bed wagon, to be used for emergency replacements on the trail.

What with helping on the blood call round-ups, riding his turn at night guard on the herd and helping Goodnight with the organization, Dusty had less time than anybody else for leisure. Yet always at the back of his mind lay the memory of the stampede and his thoughts on why it had been caused. So he kept a wary eye open for further attempts at preventing his uncle gathering enough stock to fill the contract.

"I make it five hundred and ninety, Dustine," Goodnight commented at noon on the fifth day, as they watched a further twenty steers added to the herd. "We've covered the losses, with a few over, thanks to your 'fool notion.'"

"Yes, sir," Dusty replied, flushing a little with pride at what, for Goodnight, was high praise. "No word from Mineral Wells yet though."

"It's early yet. Mark'll probably send the Kid as soon as they know something. Why don't you ride back to the ranch and see if he's come?"

"Isn't there anything I can be doing here?"

"Nothing that we can't tend to. While you're at the house, ask Rowdy if he needs any more supplies."

Dusty sat a light dun gelding he was training to take its place in his mount. The horse was still fairly fresh, but he did not rush it as he started in the direction of the main house. Riding along at a leisurely walk, he kept alert and constantly searched the surrounding country for signs of danger. His every instinct warned him that Goodnight's enemies had not given up. Not having seen anything to disturb him did nothing to lessen his suspicions.

So he came to a halt as he saw a rider appear among the bushes on a distant slope. While he had left his bed roll at the ranch house, he still carried the little Winchester carbine in the saddleboot. Reaching down, he coiled his fingers around the wrist of the carbine's butt. The rider came to a halt at this first sight of Dusty, then he removed his hat and waved it vigorously overhead. Dusty replaced the half-drawn carbine as he recognized the other.

"What's up, Spat?" Dusty inquired as they came together. "Did you find any cattle up on the north ranges?"

"A few bunches, mostly cows and yearlings like Colonel Charlie figured," Spat replied, having been sent to make a search in case the morning's attempt came to nothing.

"That won't matter," Dusty assured the other. "We've got all we need."

"Saw a feller just a short ways back."

"Know him"?"

"Nope," Spat admitted. "Way he was sneaking along, I figured he didn't want no close looking at. He wasn't a cowhand, that's for sure. Maybe an Army deserter. He was a lean cuss, wearing a sword—"

"And a buckskin shirt 'n' coonskin cap?" Dusty interrupted.

"Sure. Only he'd got a sword on his belt, and was wearing cavalry pants, so I figured—"

"You must've been riding the herd on the night before the stampede, I'd say."

"Sure I was. Why?"

"If you hadn't been, you'd likely have recognized that feller. He was one of the three who caused it."

"Damn it, Cap'n Dusty!" Spat growled, his voice brittle. "I didn't know that. When I saw how he was dressed, I took him for a deserter. Allowed he'd not want anybody to know which way he was going and stayed out of his sight rather than chance starting a shooting fuss."

Knowing the severe punishments inflicted by the Army on its recaptured deserters, Dusty appreciated Spat's point. A man desperate enough to chance going over the hill might try to kill rather than leave a witness who could guide the Army to him.

Dusty also guessed at the reason behind the brittle, wary tension shown by the cowhand. Ever since Loving's death, Spat had wondered if his motives and personal courage were in question over the incident. Although nobody had even hinted as much, Spat still wondered if things might have gone differently had he stopped to help his boss and Sid defend the cave. So Dusty had noticed a growing tendency for the cowhand to get touchy at the slightest hint, even one made unintentionally, that he might be showing undue caution in times of danger.

"You did the right thing," Dusty told him. "If there'd been shooting, we'd've wasted time and risked the herd coming out to check on it. Besides, this way we can likely track him to where he's going and find out why he's hanging around."

"You want *me* along?"

"Way I look at it, this's more than a one-man chore. And, anyways, you must be able to read sign better than I can."

"And I know where to start to look."

"Sure. Let's go."

With that Dusty allowed Spat to take the lead and they rode across the range. Keeping to cover as much as possible, Dusty followed Spat to the place where the cowhand had seen the man. Despite Spat's ideas on the matter, Dusty felt certain that the intruder had been Scroggins. No deserter—fond as he might be of the cavalry's *arme-blanche*—would retain such an obvious piece of military equipment as a saber. The weapon would attract too much attention his way.

"He come from that way," Spat said, halting and pointing to the southwest. "Herd's down there, but maybe two miles off."

"Likely he could find some place to watch us from without much chance of being seen."

"Not closer'n half a mile," Spat protested.

"That'd be close enough for him to see how we're doing," Dusty pointed out. "And if he's been around since the day of the stampede, he'll have a fair idea how well we've done."

"Where do you reckon he's going?"

"To tell his pards and his boss what he's seen. Let's see if we can find out, shall we."

"I'm all for it," Spat growled. "We owe them stinking sons-of-a-bitch something for all the extra work they've caused us."

Setting their horses moving, Dusty and Spat headed to the north. For all his earlier comments, Dusty could read sign well enough to figure the man they followed had gone out of his way to avoid being seen. After covering something over a mile, however, they found that he had put aside his caution and rode along openly.

"Likely he'd not be expecting anybody up this way," Dusty commented, "with us getting all our cattle from the south and west."

"If him or his pards know cattle, they'd figure that," Spat replied. "We combed this section for steers in the first place, to save doing any more brush-popping than we had to."

"Maybe he's not expecting being seen," Dusty said. "But we can't count on it. From now, it's us who use the cover."

The country through which they traveled offered itself ideally to unseen movement, being broken up by draws or gullies and dotted with clumps of trees.

"This's no good," Dusty remarked after a time. "We'll take too long to catch-up to him unless we can go faster. I don't want to get too far from the herd, just in case it isn't the feller I think it is."

"We can't go faster and read his sign," Spat pointed out.

"No," Dusty agreed. "Say, are there any caves up this way big enough for two or three men and their horses to hide in?"

"Never come across one, and I know this section pretty good."

"Uncle Charlie doesn't have a line cabin up here?"

"Never needed one. Hey though! There's an old mustangers' camp about two mile off, on Bluegill Creek. Just a shack, a barn and a corral, all of 'em in poor shape. Cattle don't get up that ways often enough for us to bother rebuilding."

"That'd be a good place to try looking, though," Dusty decided. "Far enough from the herd to cut the chance of any of the crew coming around. But close enough for them to keep an eye on how we're doing. We'll head up that ways and take a look."

"What if he's not there?" Spat inquired.

"Then we'll get back to the herd as fast as we can," Dusty replied. "We've got to give Uncle Charlie enough time to get ready for trouble."

Nodding in agreement, Spat changed direction and selected the shortest route to the old mustangers' camp. They rode at a faster pace, but still used caution.

Coming to a halt, Spat pointed to horse tracks crossing the route they took and joining a well-used trail. To Dusty, the story stood plain enough. Whoever had ridden that way had made a roundabout route from watching the herd. Probably he had taken a different line each day, once beyond the point they were approaching. By doing so, he would avoid leaving too plain sign of his presence in the vicinity of the cattle.

Advancing with even greater care, Dusty and Spat climbed their horses up a slope. According to the cowhand, the valley on the other side ran parallel to Bluegill Creek. Dusty knew better than to ride blithely over a rim under the prevailing conditions. So he and Spat slowed their advance and looked over before showing themselves fully. Two riders came through the trees on the opposite slope, men Dusty had good cause to remember. At a sign from the small Texan, Spat withdrew from the rim and Dusty joined him.

"One of 'em's the feller I saw, Cap'n!" the cowhand stated.

"It's Scroggins right enough," Dusty agreed. "And Turner with him."

"What're we going to do, Cap'n—?"

"Hide and jump them when they come close enough. I reckon that they can tell us some interesting stories, asked right."

Swinging from their saddles, they led the horses behind some near-by bushes. While securing his reins to a branch, Spat looked at Dusty and asked, "How do we play it, Cap'n?"

"I want at least one of them alive, both if we can," Dusty replied. "So we'll Injun up on to the rim and try to find places where they'll go between and throw down on them as they pass."

Quickly Dusty completed the fastening of his horse. He slipped the carbine from its boot. Owning only a single-shot Enfield muzzle-loader, Spat had not carried it along from the ranch house. However, he had his holstered Colt to fill his needs.

On reaching the head of the rim, they peered over cautiously. From all appearances, Turner and Scroggins intended to stick to the trail which repeated passages to and from scouting the herd had formed.

Dusty opened his mouth to tell Spat they would make their ambush where they were. The words were never said. Bringing their horses to a halt, the proposed victims turned and looked back in the direction from which they had come.

"Scrog, Al!" called a voice and a man appeared on the opposite rim, urging his horse down to where the pair waited. "You'd best come back. The boss's headed down to see us."

"Who's he?" Spat whispered.

"Luhmere," Dusty answered. "Spat, *amigo*, we're in luck."

"Do we take 'em?" asked the cowhand.

"Not from up here," Dusty decided. "As soon as we let them know we're about, they'll either fight or run. Nope, there's only one thing to do."

"I'm game for anything," the cowhand stated.

Dusty doubted if Spat would be game for what he was going to order, but went ahead just the same.

"Go get your horse and head back—"

"*Back!*" Spat growled.

"Hold it down!" Dusty hissed. "Yeah. Go back to the herd and ask Uncle Charlie to send some of the boys."

"Damn it!" Spat began. "If you reckon all I'm good for—"

"You did the right thing with Oliver Loving!" Dusty snapped back. "So, for the good Lord's sake do it right now. You know this range, which I don't. So you can get there and back faster than me."

"What're you planning to do?"

"Trail along after them—"

"We could both go."

"That's no answer, Spat. There're three of them we know about, likely another one at least brought the word about the boss coming. And I reckon he won't be traveling alone. That makes too many for us to handle without counting a whole heap too much on luck favoring us. No, we play it my way."

At any other time Spat would have admitted that Dusty made right good sense. Only the memory of how he had gone for help and left two friends to die fighting the Comanches caused him to argue. Yet he could see no wavering on Dusty's face and so gave in.

"I'll be back with the boys, Cap'n," Spat promised.

"And I'll be waiting," Dusty replied. "Take my dun and ride relay. I can handle the trailing best afoot."

Slowly, reluctantly, Spat followed Dusty from the rim. Already the other men had started to ride back up the opposite slope and were almost at the top. So Dusty was eager to get after them. In case he should lose them, he asked for and received instructions on how to locate the deserted mustangers' camp.

"Can't I—" Spat continued, after finishing his description.

"No!" Dusty stated firmly and took a box of bullets for his carbine from the dun's saddle pouches. "You're doing the only thing that'll help."

Giving a resigned shrug, Spat freed and led off the horse.

Watching the cowhand go, Dusty wondered if he should have collected more bullets for his revolvers. The paper cartridges used in the 1860 Army Colt did not travel well, stuffed into a pocket, being liable to rupture and ruin in the event of violent movement. Loading with loose powder and ball was possible, but far too slow to perform in the heat of a gunfight.

Carbine in hand, Dusty turned his thoughts to following the men. Already they had passed over the other rim and gone from sight. For all that, he advanced with care and made use of whatever cover he could find. Going up the opposite slope he found that the trio had gone beyond his range of vision. He did not try to catch up with them, knowing that to do so afoot and wearing cowhand boots—designed for riding, not hiking—would be impossible. Nor was there any need to take such measures. According to Spat's description, the trail along which the men were riding led to the deserted mustangers' camp and had, in fact, originally been made by them.

There were numerous times as he walked that Dusty cursed his boots. Yet he did not allow the increasing ache in his feet to wipe away his caution. He saw no sign of the trio but at last the camp appeared through the trees. Set on the banks of a small stream, in the open bottom of a valley, it consisted of the buildings Spat had mentioned. Beyond the stream, the wooded land started again. All of the trio's horses stood before the cabin but none of the men were in sight. From what Dusty could see, it would be inadvisable to let the other side enter the cabin. Both it and the barn had been built to last, and, while dilapidated, offered mighty effective defensive positions.

Continuing his cautious advance, Dusty decided on a change of plan. Instead of waiting for his companions to arrive, he would attempt to slip up unseen and capture the trio. Doing so would not be easy, but was preferable to letting them and whoever was coming have the cabin to hide in when Goodnight's men arrived.

About to move closer, Dusty found himself looking into the muzzle of a Sharps rifle which appeared from behind the trunk of a tree ahead of him.

FIFTEEN

I'm Going To Enjoy Making You Talk

"I told you somebody was sneaking around, Al," said Scroggins' voice from behind the rifle-sprouting tree.

"And you was right, Scrog," answered Turner, rising from behind a dogwood bush to Dusty's left and holding a Colt. "Drop the rifle, short stuff."

Like every intelligent fighting man, Dusty knew not only how but *when* to make war. Covered by two weapons and with no cover readily available on his right side, resistance would be futile and fatal. So he lowered the carbine's butt to the ground and released his hold on the barrel, letting it fall as gently as possible.

"Hey! What's the game?" Dusty asked, trying to sound mild and puzzled. "Oh! It's you fellers. Say, did you get your steers back?"

"Naw," Turner answered. "All we've got's you. Unbuckle your gunbelt and let it drop. Do it left-handed, slow and careful."

"It'd be as easy to shoot him right now," Scroggins commented.

"Like hell it would!" Turner snapped as Dusty tensed, ready to sell his life dearly. "He's Goodnight's nephew. So I'm wondering what the hell he's doing out here and afoot."

With his finger already tightening on the trigger, Scroggins frowned and halted its rearward movement.

"Get that belt off, boy!" Turner continued. "Left-handed, like I said."

The insistence on Dusty using his left hand could have cost the pair a high price. He was completely ambidextrous—a natural talent improved on in his childhood as a means of off-setting his small size—and allowed a chance, he could have just as easily and efficiently used his left hand to good advantage. He did not see the chance. Both of the men possessed sufficient gun-handling savvy to be very dangerous. So Dusty freed the pigging thongs securing the holster bottoms to his legs, unbuckled the belt and let it fall to his feet.

"That suit you?" he asked.

"Move away from it," Turner ordered and, as Dusty obeyed, went on, "Now put your hands behind you."

Coming to a halt, Dusty did as he was instructed. However, he placed his wrists together instead of crossing them. Without presenting Dusty with the opportunity to resist, Turned moved in behind him. Holstering his Colt, the man drew a length of cord from his pocket. He formed a loop, hooked it up over Dusty's hands, drew it tight and started to fasten it without making the small Texan cross his wrists.

"That's got him," Turner grinned, walking confidently by the prisoner. "Let's take him down to the cabin and ask him some questions."

"What if I don't answer?" Dusty inquired.

"I sure hope you don't," Turner told him. "I'm going to enjoy making you talk. Get moving."

Not until Dusty's hands were secured did Scroggins relax.

"Hey, Al!" the lanky man said. "He's got a Henry, only it looks better'n any Henry I ever saw."

"It's your'n," Turner told him generously, then looked at Dusty. "Come on."

"How do you figure to make me?" the small Texan drawled, watching Scroggins lean the Sharps against a tree and make for the carbine. "You can't use your gun in case I've got pards around looking for me."

"We don't need guns to handle a runt like you," Turner spat back.

"You didn't do so good last time," Dusty pointed out. "And there was three of you at it then."

A hot flush of annoyance crept over Turner's face. With the plan they had been instructed in only partially successful—not even that, according to what he had seen of Goodnight's herd growing in numbers— Turner's employers were vocal in their recriminations. Worse than that, they flatly refused to pay the trio until some more adequate result was forthcoming. That their failure had been brought about by such a small, insignificant cuss increased Turner's anger.

"One of us'll be enough!" Turner snarled and moved toward Dusty. "See if it ain't."

Facing Dusty, but to his right, Turner prepared to enforce his demands. Catching the small Texan's right bicep with his left hand, Turner began to pull him forward and drew back his own left fist for a punch. Just an instant too late the man became aware of the size and solid nature of the muscles he gripped. Yet he still did not realize that he was playing right into his "victim's" hands.

Dusty did not try to hold back against the pull. Instead he let himself be drawn toward Turner. Up close enough for his purpose, Dusty pivoted on his right foot until its toe pointed directly at Turner. Whipping up his left leg, Dusty propelled its knee with considerable force between the other's spread-apart lower limbs. Turner let out a croaking cry of pure agony. Stumbling back and doubling over, Turner collapsed writhing to the ground.

Becoming aware of what was happening, Scroggins forgot his interest in the new model "Henry" and turned. Just in time he remembered the need for reasonable silence and decided against using the carbine as a firearm. There seemed no need to shoot when dealing with a small man whose hands were tied behind his back; even if he was fortunate enough to have done Turner a severe piece of no good. Striding forward, he swung up the little Winchester in both hands, his intention being to drive its metal-shod butt against the back of Dusty's head.

Anticipating the attack and gambling on the way that it would come, Dusty was ready to counter it. From kneeing Turner, he brought his left foot back to the ground. With the carbine swinging savagely in his direction, he bowed his torso forward. Over his head whistled the butt and he felt the wind of its passing. Still bent over, he twisted his hips slightly, balanced on the left leg and shot his right foot in Scroggins' direction. The high-heeled boot spiked hard into the lanky man's belly as he continued forward with the weight of his abortive blow. Although the kick landed just a touch too high to be fully effective, it threw its recipient backward. Reeling under the impact, Scroggins dropped the carbine but did not go down.

Ignoring Scroggins for a moment, Dusty brought down his leg. Before him, Turner was still rolling in torment and clutching at the injured area. Dusty could not take the chance of the man staying incapacitated while he dealt with Scroggins. So he sprang forward and kicked Turner at the side of the jaw. Rolled over by the force of the latest attack, Turner came to rest on his back and lay without a movement.

Whirling around, Dusty faced Scroggins. Pride prevented the lean man from yelling for help. Scroggins could imagine Luhmere's comments if called to help against the small, handicapped Texan.

"All right, feller!" Scroggins snarled, sliding his saber from its sheath. "I'm going to cut you to doll-rags."

From the way Scroggins advanced, he knew more than the rudiments of handling a saber. Bounding in, he launched an inside swing at Dusty's head. If he had been dealing with the normal run of cowhand, Scroggins would have been successful. However, Dusty had received saber training from childhood and still managed to keep up his practice when at home. He avoided the attack by a rapid stride to the rear. Scroggins followed the small Texan, making cuts that Dusty identified before they started and evaded by fast footwork. Yet Scroggins managed to keep himself at a distance where Dusty could not reach him with a kick. It was, Dusty knew, only a matter of time before Luhmere made an appearance to see what was delaying his companions' return. Somehow Dusty must deal with his assailant, free his hands and arm himself before that happened.

Being missed by a savage down-lashing direct swing

to the head, Dusty appeared to land awkwardly. Stumbling, he fell with his back to the trunk of a sturdy cottonwood tree. With a snarl of satisfaction, Scroggins followed up his advantage. Forward shot the saber in a near classic lunge, its point aimed at the small Texan's belly. At the last instant Dusty twisted himself aside. Hissing by him, the point of the saber spiked deep into the wood. Once again the impetus of an attack carried Scroggins into danger. Thrusting himself from the tree, Dusty met the man. Driving up his knee, Dusty slammed it into Scroggins' chest. Staggering back, he straightened up. Dusty followed him, bounding into the air and sending both boots crashing into him. The right foot caught the center of Scroggins' chest and the left impacted on his jaw. Lifted from his feet by the force of the *mae-tobigeri* forward jump kick of *karate*, Scroggins crashed to the springy turf. He bounced once and then went limply still.

Landing from his attack, Dusty staggered and caught his balance. There was no time to waste, but he looked around him and made sure that he did not need fear a further attack from his assailants or Luhmere. Satisfied on that score, he went to the cottonwood. Turning with his back to the tree, he carefully hooked his bound hands under the saber. Then he rested the small of his back against the hilt, pressing on it in an attempt to hold it firm. Raising his hands slowly, he felt the touch of cold steel on his flesh. At that moment the wisdom of avoiding crossing his wrists showed. Edging his hands back and forwards, Dusty felt the saber's cutting edge slitting the fibers of the cord.

Having no wish to slice open his hands, Dusty worked slowly and carefully. The need to hurry soon rose. Rolling on to his face, Scroggins slowly forced himself up on to hands and knees. Beyond him, Turner was groaning and stirring. As the sound reached his ears, Scroggins looked toward its source. He shook his head to clear the swirling mists from it and remembrance returned with a rush. At the sight of Dusty standing against the tree, fury twisted Scroggins' face. Spitting out a curse, he grabbed at his holstered revolver.

With a tug, Dusty snapped the remaining strands of the rope. From doing so, his right hand slipped into the saber's hilt. Giving a pull which plucked the point from the tree's trunk, Dusty thrust himself into motion. While he could claim to be something of an expert in the use of the saber, the attack he launched did not come from the curriculum of any *salle-de-armes*. Leaving the tree's shelter, Dusty threw himself forward in a somersaulting dive. Going by the kneeling Scroggins, Dusty launched a slash in mid-air. Steel sliced into the side of the man's neck until the cutting edge chipped against the neck bones. The Colt was only just clearing leather as Dusty struck, Scroggins' reactions being too sluggish for the rapid movement which would have saved him. Feeling the saber stick, Dusty released it. Ahead of him lay his carbine. Never had he felt so pleased than when his hands closed on the walnut furnishings and he finished his roll holding the fully loaded Winchester.

Twisting around on his knees, Dusty halted the carbine halfway to his shoulder. Scroggins sprawled on his back, dripping his lifeblood over the springy grass. That left Turner, and Dusty swung his way. Still too hurt and dazed to intervene, the man offered no immediate danger. Under the circumstances, however, Dusty did not dare take a chance. Not when Turner might recover sufficiently to take cards before Dusty could deal with the last of the trio. Dusty rose and approached the groaning hardcase. A sharp blow from the carbine's butt tumbled Turner back into harmless unconsciousness.

For a moment Dusty stood breathing hard. Then he mopped his brow with a bandana. Crossing to where his gunbelt lay, he picked it up and strapped it on.

"Now for Luhmere," he breathed. "Whooee! I wouldn't want to go through that again in a hurry—or ever."

It was, he knew, as tight a spot as he had ever been in. Once more he had reason to be thankful for his small size, insignificant appearance and the *karate* lessons received from Tommy Okasi.

Fully armed again, Dusty went to the top of the slope and took his first long look at the mustangers' camp. The cabin, with the horses before it, was closest to his position. Without a time-consuming detour, he could not make use of the barn or corral as a means of concealment. While he could reach the foot of the slope unseen, he faced crossing some sixty yards of open ground from there to his destination.

Running would make too much noise and was certain to disturb the three horses. By approaching at an apparently leisurely walk, he might hope that Luhmere thought it was one of his companions returning. The horses were less likely to take fright and raise an alarm at the sight of a walking man.

Carbine held before him ready for use, Dusty advanced from behind the last of the trees. He was at an angle from the front of the building. Its windows had boards across them, with spaces between which the barrel of a weapon could be lined. However, the builder had done his work well. Search as minutely as he might, Dusty could see no place in the walls where the chinking had fallen from between the logs sufficiently to allow Luhmere to fire on him through the gap.

The horses out front presented the greatest danger, but they stood with their rumps to him. Walking as gently as if crossing over eggshells on top of Ketchum grenades,* Dusty hoped to remain undetected.

Step by step Dusty drew nearer to the cabin. Still Luhmere showed no hint of knowing of his presence. Twenty yards from the building, he wondered if he should continue the walk or stake all in a sudden dash.

Faintly he heard the sound of horses' hooves on the other slope. Looking up, he saw four men riding through the trees and downward. Although three of them wore range clothes, the fourth was a heavily built dude whom Goodnight would have recognized as one of his rivals for the Army contract. Dusty did not identify the man as such, but figured who he must be from the shouted conversation heard earlier between Luhmere, Turner and Scroggins. From their reactions, Dusty decided that at least some of the newcomers knew him.

Reining in their horses, they stared into the valley and one of the range men yelled, "It's the runt that was with Goodnight!"

"Runt nothing," a second westerner went on, grabbing for his revolver. "He's Dusty Fog."

"It's sure nice to be well known!" Dusty breathed, starting to swing the carbine to his shoulder.

Although the second speaker drew fast, he was beyond any range at which a revolver could hope to make a hit. Which did not prevent him from trying. Coming out, his Colt cracked. Where its bullet went

---

*For description of a Ketchum Hand Grenade, read *Cold Deck, Hot Lead*.

did not concern Dusty. Cradling the carbine against his shoulder, he began to take aim at his attacker.

"Get him!" screeched the dude. "Where the hell are you Luhmere?"

A question which Dusty could have answered. Before he could line his sights and squeeze the trigger, he saw the cabin's front door bust open. Revolver in hand, Luhmere lunged into the open. At the sight of Dusty, Luhmere swung around and tried to throw down on him. Changing his aim, Dusty touched off a shot at the exact moment Luhmere let his Colt's hammer fall. Luhmere's bullet missed Dusty by a couple of inches. The small Texan's struck the other man in the body. Reeling under the impact of the flat-nosed piece of lead, Luhmere disappeared into the cabin.

Down the slope raced the men, firing as they came. So far they were using only their revolvers and were not aided by sitting fast-running horses. Dusty knew that their aim would improve as the range decreased. Blurring the carbine's lever through its reloading cycle, Dusty leapt toward the cabin. Flying lead churned into the wood, throwing splinters just above his head. Then he was hidden from the newcomers by the side of the building. Halting, he raised the carbine and thrust it around the corner to sight at the nearest of the four men.

The horses were snorting and fighting against their reins, but Dusty heard another sound. Turning his head, he saw Luhmere coming from the cabin. Blood was running down the man's shirt, but he still held his revolver and was clearly well enough to use it.

With the carbine's barrel extended beyond the end of the building, Dusty knew he could not hope to withdraw and turn it fast enough to save himself. So he did not try. Instead he released it and threw himself backward with hands fanning across to his Colts. Luhmere's gun roared, but he was still aiming at where Dusty had been standing and so missed. Landing on his back, Dusty cut loose with both his revolvers. Angling up and inward, the bullets ripped through Luhmere's left breast barely an inch apart. Slammed backward, the man once more disappeared into the cabin. This time Dusty did not expect to see him come out.

By that time the riders had reached the far side of the stream and Dusty landed in plain sight of them. Starting to sit up, he felt the hat torn from his head by a bullet. Knowing the deadly gun skill of the man they faced, the three range-raised riders reined in their horses. Either Wednesbury failed to recognize the danger, or had less control of his mount. Whatever the reason, he plunged into the water waving his revolver and heading across. Suddenly, for no apparent reason it seemed, the dude jolted back and slid sideways from his saddle. As he splashed into lhe stream, the deep crack of a Spencer carbine pounded on the rim at the side he approached.

More shots blasted from behind Dusty and he could see the consternation which rose among the attacking trio. One of them tumbled from his horse and the last two set their mounts galloping, headed back the way they had come as fast as they could go. They were speeded on their way by the wild "Yeeah!" rebel war yell Dusty knew all too well.

Standing up, Dusty looked to where Red Blaze and Spat were running toward him followed by five more of the Swinging G's cowhands.

"Are you all right, Dusty?" Red asked.

"Sure," the small Texan replied and looked wryly at his bullet-holed new Stetson. "But this's the roughest section on hats I've ever seen."

SIXTEEN

They Won't Have Time To Try Again

"Wednesbury's his name," Goodnight said as he and the sheriff of Young County looked at the dude's body. "He was one of the pair who had bid against me for the Army beef contract."

"And they've been trying every damned which ways to stop Uncle Charlie getting enough cattle to fill it," Red went on.

"Can you prove that?" Sheriff Kater inquired.

"Not in a way we could put before a judge and jury," Dusty replied before his impulsive cousin could speak.

It was noon on the day after the fight and the sheriff had been fetched out from Graham to learn of it. After examining the sign at the scene of Dusty's capture and around the cabin, Kater was inspecting the bodies and asking his questions. Red went on to tell how one of the cowhands had discovered tracks which proved that somebody had been watching them working. So Goodnight had sent Red and five men to track down and if possible capture the snooper. On the way, they had met Spat who led them to their goal. Nearing the camp, Red displayed the cool capability so few people suspected. He ordered the men to leave their horses and make the rest of the journey on foot. Drawing near to the valley, they had arrived just in time to give Dusty a badly needed hand.

"Turner talked when he come around and found himself at the Swinging G house," Dusty went on. "Not that he knew much. Luhmere was the big augur for the three, he was the only one real close to the bosses and never told the other two more than he needed. As far as I can tell, the idea was formed when their bosses learned about Pitzer losing the herd. They knew what kind of man Chisum was and figured he'd turn on Uncle Charlie if he was paid well enough—"

"I'd like to think Chisum didn't know about the rest of the game," Goodnight put in, "and allowed all they wanted was to stop me gettin; enough cattle together to fill the contract."

"Maybe that's all he knew," Dusty drawled. "He went along, anyways. Only we heard how he got the herd earlier than they figured, thanks to Dawn. So the cattle weren't mixed with your stuff when Luhmere brought Wardle and the other ranchers. I'll bet that none of Chisum's crew'd've come out from Graham if all had gone as it was supposed to, so's they'd not be around when the shooting started. Turner says that he, Scroggins and Luhmere sat clear of the others ready to pull out *pronto* when Wardle got the powder burning. Only Wardle didn't, so Luhmere made a crack at starting it himself."

"Only you stopped him," Kater commented.

"Not well enough," Dusty answered. "Turner allows that they found this camp and Luhmere left him here with Scroggins to watch how we got on, then went to meet up with their bosses, but doesn't know where. When Luhmere got back, he said they wouldn't get paid unless they did a better job at scattering the herd. The two of them were coming to see if they could figure on a way of doing it when Luhmere got word the boss was coming. Feller who told him went back to fetch Wednesbury along and Luhmere collected his pards. Scroggins either saw or heard me following and they caught me. Only I spoiled their game."

"Does Turner know who helped those three fellers bust out of my jail?" asked the sheriff.

"No," Dusty replied. "I reckon it was Targue, when he pretended to go for Chisum, but I can't prove it."

"Do you want me to do anything, Charlie?" Kater inquired.

"Not unless you want to. And it'd likely be a waste of time trying. Wednesbury's partner'd deny all knowledge and we can't prove he had any."

"Those two fellers who run out kept going," Red remarked. "Even if they tell Wednesbury's pard what's happened, they won't have time to try again."

"We'll be moving out in two days, Wade," Goodnight explained. "I've got my herd gathered and word came in afore we left the spread this morning that the Mineral Wells men and cattle'll be here today. Given a touch of luck, I'll be waiting at Fort Sumner when Wednesbury's partner arrives. We'll settle things any way he wants when he gets there."

"It's your play, Charlie," Kater stated. "I'll tend to things at this end. On my way back, I'll collect Turner and take him to jail. I reckon you've got things to do."

"I have," Goodnight agreed. "Dustine, Charles,

come with me. You boys stay and help the sheriff."

By the time they reached the vicinity of the lake, they saw the Mineral Wells stock being driven toward the shipping herd. A faint smile played on Goodnight's face at the sight. The means to make his dream come true were at hand. Then the smile faded. Wednesbury was dead, but his partner remained alive and active. There might be other attempts to prevent Goodnight from delivering the herd to Fort Sumner.